Men in their Passions

Other published works by John Roman Baker

The Drift of Time
No Fixed Ground
The Paris Syndrome
The Vicious Age
2020

The Nick & Greg Books
Nick & Greg
Time of Obsessions
Nick's House
Greg in Paris
Love & Cowardice
Nick's Fugue
Greg at the Station

Other Novels
The Dark Antagonist
The Sea and the City

Short Stories
Brighton Darkness

Plays
The Crying Celibate Tears Trilogy
The Prostitution Plays
Prisoners of Sex

Poetry
Cast Down
The Deserted Shore
Gethsemane
Poèmes à Tristan

Men in their Passions

part of the series
The Drift of Time
by
John Roman Baker

WILKINSON HOUSE

Men in their Passions
by John Roman Baker

Copyright © John Roman Baker 2025

The moral right of the author has been asserted.
Published by Wilkinson House Ltd, August 2025

FIRST EDITION
978-1-899713-74-5

Wilkinson House Ltd.,
20-22 Wenlock Road,
London, N1 7GU
United Kingdom

www.wilkinsonhouse.com
wilkinsonhousebooks@gmail.com

Cover image: Raphael, *Fire in the Borgo* (detail)

British Library Cataloguing-in-Publication Data
A catalogue record for this book is available
from the British Library.

1

This is all recollection. I had left Paris for good, and returned to Brighton in 1970 to recover from all the ills that I had suffered in France. I felt that my body was scarred with the passions I had lived through: too many men, one after another, and yet none of them gave me what I searched for. A real connection. A real caring.

I recollected them to forget them: the bisexual man who loved me, but also had sex with other men for money; the student whom I loved the most, but our time together was short; the businessman who showed me foreign places and took me on trips to Spain, Portugal and finally down to Greece. I liked him but did not love him, and he resented me and left me. These were followed by a young writer, mystical in his views of life and again bisexual. Sex with him was limited because he avoided anal sex and any real close intimacy. And finally, before my departure, a young man met in a Paris gay club, and a love relationship that was brutal. He often hit me as he made love to me. This continued for as long as I could stand it, and then I decided to take the ship back to England. I was tired.

All through these years, I had taught English at a small private school.

2

The first night back, I slept in a guest house. The following day, I saw an advertisement for a room to let in Dorset Gardens. Time has erased the number, but the two men who opened the door, smiled at me, invited me in, and led me into a cluttered room. All this I can recall clearly. The clutter consisted of too many well-upholstered chairs for such a small living room, two budgerigars in a cage in one corner, and in another, a large writing desk open and spilling with papers. It was so full that envelopes and letters lay scattered around on the heavy carpet. One of the men, younger than the other, bent down and crammed the mess back into the desk.

"I'm such a messy person," he said.

"Yes, Derek, you are," commented the older man smiling indulgently. Then he turned to me and said, "I am Andrew, and this is my partner, Derek. Would you like to sit down?"

I sat on one of the chairs.

Andrew turned back to Derek and in the softest voice said, "Would you make us a pot of tea? I sense this young man is thirsty."

"No, really—"

"Nonsense. It's a hot day. You need refreshment. If you are going to live here, then you must experience our small domestic ways. I hope you are not disturbed by our—how shall I put it—orientation? This word *gay* crops up. I am not a fan of it."

"I prefer same-sex lovers," Derek said and gave me a look which I could only interpret as being flirtatious. He winked at me, and his eyes were bright and enthusiastic.

"This young man is very good-looking," Andrew said. "Get

over the fact, Derek. Now, will you please make some tea?"

Derek dutifully left the room.

"He loves beautiful faces," Andrew said, seating himself at a distance on another chair.

"Now, your name is—?" he asked.

"Jean-Paul," I replied.

"How very French. Your English accent is perfect."

"My mother, now dead, was French. My father was English. He is also dead."

"God bless them," Andrew replied. "So young to bear such grief. I am forty-five, and mine are alive. I couldn't live without them."

"You are very fortunate," and with my sentence finished, Andrew stared at me, perhaps analysing me to see if I was an appropriate tenant.

"Would you like a room in our house?" he eventually asked.

"I would."

"Why?"

"Because I think you are good people."

"Flatterer! But charming. French manners, no doubt. How can one resist?"

"What?" I asked.

"Such a touch of class."

"Thank you."

Derek came into the room and there was a short ceremony of drinking from flower-patterned cups.

"Derek likes you, which is obvious, and I like you, so I see no reason why we shouldn't get into that nasty and rather vulgar thing called business."

I agreed to the weekly sum, and after a few more questions about France and why I had left it, the meeting came to an end. Before leaving, I mentioned, as if in passing, that I liked men myself.

3

The room was pleasant. It had a single bed, a wardrobe, and a table with two chairs. They had even managed to get a two-seater sofa into the room. I arranged the small collection of books I had brought back from Paris, and taking money from the bank, I bought a record player. I discovered composers I had not heard before. One of them was Bartok. I played his music low, but one day Derek knocked on the door and asked what the music was. I replied that it was Bartok's *Music for Strings, Percussion and Celesta*. He sat with me for a while and listened to it.

Occasionally they invited me down to tea. The conversation was generally a one-sided one. They wanted to know about Paris, and I gave a censored version of my life. Maybe it was rude, or perhaps just tactful, but I never questioned them about their lives. They didn't mind. They liked me. And they often repeated that I had such good manners. I just smiled and responded to further questions.

In my room, hidden under a pile of books, I had drawings by an artist I had known in Paris. He had said he could draw any fantasy for me, and was not shocked when I asked him to draw naked images of Jesus and John together. It took him a week to draw them, and he added a third person. I asked why. He replied by saying, "To add a bit of spice, I have included naughty Judas. Judas is the horniest. He likes to cum, watching them." The way he drew him, Judas was very handsome: a youth of angelic beauty. His penis was larger than either Jesus or John's, and his almost childlike face added to my excitement. The artist had been a friend of Jean Cocteau, had seen his explicit drawings, and in a more detailed style, now drew erotic images for all too ready buyers. Call it a fetish, call it a perversity, this fulfilled my masturbatory desires. I was baptised a Catholic, and even as a child, I thought Jesus and John must have been really close, and during puberty I masturbated believing they were lovers. I never referred to Jesus as Christ. I believed in his loving and his good words, but not in his belief of a heaven or God the Father or resurrection.

During my time in the Dorset Gardens house, I masturbated a lot. I never went to bars. Derek had recommended a club near the old Police Station, and I thought that was so funny I did not believe him.

"We are not against the law anymore," he said sternly, and sighing, added, "You really *have* been away from this country a long time. As long as we do it in private, it's fine."

Despite this news, which I already knew, I still felt awkward about the Brighton bars and clubs. In Paris it had been different. Four of the lovers I had lived with I had met in a basement club near to Saint-Germain-des-Pres. I felt free there from Britain's barbaric laws.

I secluded myself and wrote (I had one novel published) and to relax after writing I looked at the drawings. I liked Jesus's passivity. The artist had drawn him in such a way that he always had an ecstatic look on his face. John was the active partner, and Judas was the voyeur, like me, enjoying it all. As I washed my body in the bathroom, I often felt bad about myself. Was I sick in my mind?

The room was closing in on me. I had to get out more.

4

The woman who told fortunes on the pier was not there, and the little steps that led up to the clairvoyant's hut displayed a closed sign. For no reason I could think of, I wanted to know what was in store for me, and anyway, it was good in itself to get out of the room I now referred to as my cage. I returned often and one day found the door of the hut was open. I caught my breath, hesitated, and then shrugged my shoulders and looked upwards. The sky was a bright blue, and below I could hear the slightly choppy sea. A wind was blowing from the East, but there was no evidence of approaching clouds. There were surprisingly few people on the pier for a Saturday, and the numerous hungry seagulls overhead were out of luck. Before I saw the open door, I was planning to go into the arcade to push pennies, and to allow myself the juvenile pleasure of seeing (yet again) *What the Butler Saw*. To my surprise, the thought had given me an erection. I turned away from the arcade and ascended the few steps to the hut.

"Hello?" I called.

The door was only half-open and the part of the interior that I could see was in semi-darkness. I repeated my hello and out of the dim space within, an elderly man appeared.

"I'm looking for a reading." I paused. I did not like the look on the man's face.

"I am replacing my colleague today. She is unwell. If you wait a moment I will set things up."

I remained standing at the entrance still hesitant about entering.

"You can come in now."

His voice was thin and reedy. There was a whistle in the

sound. I made my decision and entered. Inside, the only light came from three candles on a ledge beside a table. The man was seated in front of it, and with a gesture he motioned for me to sit on the rickety wooden chair facing him.

"I would like you to shuffle these cards," he said, handing me the pack. "When you have finished I would like you to place six cards in front of me, and a seventh one to the side."

"Why six?" I asked.

"That is not for you to know," he replied.

"And the seventh?"

"That is the final card. I can tell you that the seventh is either the future or the past."

I placed the cards face downwards and he turned them over one by one, very slowly. The seventh he did not touch.

"You are alone," he said slowly. "I see many faces, and they are looking sideways. They do not want to look at you."

I suddenly felt cold and wanted to leave.

"I have never been alone," I replied.

"Ah, but you were. All men. It was a false closeness. There was a vast distance between all of them and you."

"I don't understand," I murmured.

"This is what I see in the cards. You are in your mid-twenties, and you have never known love. Or should I say, you have known only the semblance of it." He paused, then briefly looking at me, said, "You have had multiple lovers. The cards are crowded with names. A human jungle of them. I do not approve of what I see. I think perhaps you should have chosen another clairvoyant."

His voice was full of contempt.

"But there is more to me than those men," I replied.

There was a smell of decay in the hut.

"Is there?"

"I think so."

"If your thoughts were good, I would agree with you."

He accentuated his words with a sort of growl. Outside the cry of the seagulls grew louder, and I could hear the waves slap more loudly against the pier. Was it the approach of a storm?

"I have very little else to say," he said. "If you don't change your ways, you are lost. In fact, you may be lost already. Even before entering this hut you were having obscene thoughts."

I was not going to endure these insults any longer and I shouted at him.

"You know nothing about me. And what of the seventh card? Aren't you even going to look at it?"

He was not touched by my anger and he turned the seventh card slowly over.

"I have nothing to add. Nothing I want to add. I can only say that the card says there is nothing of any good in your life, past or present."

"Liar!" I said.

"Does a mirror that reflects nothing have meaning?" he asked. He threw the cards to the floor. "I want no money for this reading. Now get out. I am filled with disgust."

I did as he said and stumbled down the steps. A good-looking young man, standing at the entrance to the arcade, was looking at me. I heard the hut door slam behind me. The waves were now lashing at the pier and the wooden slats shook. I felt very hot and I fainted.

5

The same young man who had been staring at me was now dabbing my face and neck with water. I was leaning back in a deckchair and tried to look up at him. The glare of the sun was too bright, and I could barely see his features. The only aspect of him I saw in this haze of giddy light was what I perceived to be an orange halo around his head. As the mist cleared in my mind and my eyes gained strength, I was aware of his abundant red hair.

"I am better," I whispered, and lowering his head close to mine, he brushed his lips across my forehead. His lips were cold.

"Did he give you a bad time?" he whispered back.

"Yes, but—"

"But what?"

"I never faint. This is the first time."

"It happens," he replied, and then quite suddenly I was aware all too sharply of objects and of people. A group of women were looking at us, close by. I stared into his eyes. From one second to the next they changed from brown to green.

"Your eyes are—"

"Slightly different," he said. "One is closer to brown than the other, which is green. It can be disconcerting."

He then moved back and stood over me. His slim body and unlined face revealed that he was younger than me. I asked him how old he was.

"Twenty."

"And your name?"

"Joseph. And yours?"

"Jean-Paul."

He smiled. A sleek smile. A knowing smile, as if he knew that already.

"Well, Jean-Paul, are you steady enough on your feet now to walk to the exit?"

I felt giddy as I got up. Joseph clasped my arm to steady me, and with small steps I began to walk. It was as if I had received a great blow. There was a pain in my chest.

"You need a drink," he said.

We made it to the exit and crossed over to the Royal Albion Hotel. He suggested we find somewhere to sit down as soon as possible.

"East Street," I murmured. "There's a place there."

"Are you sure you are well enough? The Albion has a bar."

"I don't like hotels," I replied, lying to him, and I did not know why. In France I'd stayed in many hotels. I looked at Joseph's face. He reminded me of a former lover who had also liked hotels, not in looks, but in his manner of talking. For some reason I had forgotten the man's name.

"You remind me of someone," I said as we walked.

"A good person, I hope," he replied.

As we entered East Street, I felt faint again.

"Talk to me," I said. "Talk to me about anything. Keep this panic at bay. It was panic back there on the pier. That man."

"He is a charlatan. I went to him once. He told me such a lot of nonsense. You were clearly susceptible to his nastiness. He was nasty to me as well. He told me he saw the devil in the seventh card."

"He refused to tell me what he could see in the seventh card," I replied.

"According to him, it was in the seventh card that the devil chose to be present, and the devil was going to leap at me from it. Can you imagine that? A charlatan. He likes to destroy *us*."

"Who is *us*?" I asked.

"Men like us," he replied. And then in the street he kissed me on the mouth. It was a long kiss, and the taste of his saliva was bitter.

6

In the pub he drank a lot; a quiet succession of glasses of vodka. I drank a glass of wine, but I realised, and I don't know why, that he did not get drunk; that he was incapable of getting drunk. The more I looked at his face, I wondered who he was. What he was really like inside.

"You are analysing me," he said, and pressed my knee with his hand.

"I was thinking of that card. The seventh."

"The devil? Do you believe in the devil?"

"It's alright, Joseph, we don't have to talk about this." It was the first time I had called him by his name. Then, as if it was someone else speaking, I said, "You are beautiful. Really beautiful, and yet—"

"What?"

"I'm not sure."

"You've just met me. I am at this moment whatever you want me to be."

I stared at him in silence. Was this young man dangerous? Should I walk out now?

"You are undecided about me," he said.

I looked at him again. I felt disturbed.

"We can't go further than this," I said.

"Further than what?"

"This sudden intensity. This meeting."

"Why? I want you."

"No good can come of it," I replied.

"It will be good. I promise," and he reached over and caressed my face. "I need a friend."

"I am alone."

"No longer."

"Joseph, I will meet you here in a week's time. I have to reflect on all this."

Joseph stood up. He held out his hand, and I reached out and shook it. His grip was firm.

"I will be here in a week's time, at the same hour as now. If you are not here, I will leave you to yourself. I will leave you to your aloneness."

He walked out of the pub, and I felt another stab in my chest. I drank the last of the vodka he had left in his glass and licked the rim of the glass. I imagined his lips. They were cold, but I wanted that cold. Could this be the beginning of love? I wondered. Then the thought faded into a moment of frightening and irrational joy. I felt him holding me up, holding me upwards, out of this world. Then I fell to earth. I fell into myself.

"I won't see him again," I said aloud as I walked along East Street, towards the sea.

7

I was there on time at the pub the following week. The barman recognised me and said he had a letter for me. I took it, my hands trembling, and ripped it open.

Jean-Paul,
I have gone to Venice. Someone invited there for four days. He'll pay me to paint his portrait. That's what I do—portraits. Will we meet again? Who knows?
Joseph

I felt relieved. I felt safe. Those few lines had rescued me, and yet, perversely inside of me, a voice said, you want him. I went outside into the street and the voice was still there insisting, you want me very badly, and I literally heard Joseph's voice. There was laughter in it.

8

It was time for me to move from Dorset Gardens. An apathy had set in. I stayed in my room a lot at the time, thinking and pondering the life I had led in Paris; all of the crimes of the heart that had been committed there. I gave in my notice to leave.

"Aren't you happy here?" they asked.

"I like you both, but I must move on."

"Let's talk it over with some tea and cakes."

"There isn't much I can say."

"Are you sure?"

"Very sure."

"We know it can't be seventh heaven being shut up in that room for so many hours. It's not good to be alone."

"I've been content enough."

"Ah, but that's not happiness, is it?"

"Contentment can often be better. I guess I am just restless to move on."

"You must think this over. Now, let's have something to eat."

"Yes." I laughed. "I haven't told you that I've been writing. At the moment it's not going too well."

"Oh, do tell us what it's about."

"I am attempting a second novel, but the attempt is failing."

They poured me a cup of tea, and Derek brought in a plate of cakes. They asked me to have one.

"I have a lot of stress in my stomach."

"Oh, it's the thought of losing one's figure, isn't it? We know the feeling. But cakes can give you a sort of uplift. The sensation they give in the mouth can be a joy in itself."

I took one of the cakes, put it on my plate and looked at it. It was oozing too much cream and disgusted me. Then I heard a big sigh from both of them.

"To think, it is 1970! How time passes."

This observation was made by one of the two, but I cannot recall which of the two it was. The one who had not spoken added the words, "Yes, time passes. It has to. We can't stop the clocks."

"Oh no," the other chuckled. "Youth could never grow if we did. It would be a crime to stop the clocks. But still, it is 1970 and yet I recall the days of 1950 so often. No idea why. Maybe it's because the plays at the Theatre Royal were so funny. The 1950s were a fun time, except for those stupid laws."

I said nothing. As a child I remembered watching awful plays there.

"I like the theatre," I said.

"Do tell. What was the last play you saw?"

"It was a play in Paris. Claudel. *Partage du midi.* Edwige Feuillère was in it."

"We are very ignorant. We have never heard of either the actress or the play."

"I'm not sure her English would be good enough for the Theatre Royal," I replied.

"I like a laugh," and both of them said it in chorus, and the conversation ended. Eventually I was ushered out of the living room with the elaborate gesture of a ringed hand.

9

The first time I went to a gay nightclub, I saw Joseph. It was the club near the old police station. He was dressed in a black suit which contrasted well with his red hair. At first, he pretended not to see me. A game men often played with me in Paris. Then, quite suddenly, he was all over me, like an enthusiastic puppy.

"How was Venice?" I asked coldly.

He had stopped licking my face and his green/brown eyes looked at me in amazement, not real amazement, but the put-on look that gives the same effect.

"That was ages ago," he replied.

"I got your letter. They handed it to me at the pub."

"Oh, yes, I hoped they might," he said vaguely. "Now, can I buy you a drink?"

"Thank you. I'll have vodka."

"I thought you didn't drink vodka."

"I have become a closet vodka drinker. I always think of you when I have one."

"You're laughing at me."

"Probably."

His slim, black figure, marched across the less than vast space of the club, and he returned with the drinks. I downed mine in one go. In fact, I had become a secret drinker. The room in Dorset Gardens, which I had not yet left, was driving me to alcohol and blissful forgetfulness. I had not yet found a suitable place to live.

"I don't want you to become an alcoholic," Joseph said.

"I won't."

"It can creep up on you," he replied.

"So can love, Joseph, and like love one can try to resist it."

He ignored this and carried on talking, but I was not listening. I went into a sort of trance. I saw a wall of paintings. I saw the real joy of mankind in them; the giving and the taking. I knew it had nothing to do with so-called religious art. It was not like the Giottos in Assisi. It was not like the Piero della Francescas in Florence. It was something else. Something that I could not describe, and then with a blink of my eyes, the vision was gone. I came out of the trance.

"Do you have money?" Joseph asked.

"Why?"

"I need to know. Money is its own bargaining chip. All of us, male or female, have a price tag."

"Yes, I have money," I replied quietly.

"Oh, do you get much financial return from it?"

"I'm not really concerned about that. A relative died. A cousin I never met, left what he had to me. It's strange how people behave. I wish I had met him."

"How kind he was," and there was a sardonic note in his voice as he said the words.

"I've made up my mind about you, Joseph. I want you."

We were sitting side by side, and Joseph put his big red hand on my thigh. My right thigh. The touch burnt into me.

"What is it, Jean-Paul? You look hot. Have I heated you up? So, will you come live with me and be my—?" and he paused, and laughed.

"Finish it," I said, and pushed away his hand.

"I can't finish it. It comes from a poem, I think. Come live with me and be—something."

"I will live with you," I said.

The temptation was too great, and yet at the same time I felt that I was falling apart.

He got up and bought us both double vodkas.

"I want to get drunk," he said, "but I know I never will. If I got drunk, all the inside of me would be open to you. What horrors and delights you would see."

"Or maybe love?" I replied.

He smiled at me. It was a mocking smile, and his beauty was accentuated by it. The golden halo surrounding his handsome head almost blinded me. He was like the sun, and you should not look directly at the sun.

10

An imaginary dialogue played out in my head.

"I have had other lovers in my life," I said.

Joseph stared at me in silence, then he spoke.

"What can I say to that?"

"Say nothing."

"But you expect me to say something. To be surprised?" Again there was laughter in his voice.

"Say nothing. And anyway, you can't reply."

I looked into his eyes. They were empty.

"You're wrong, I could say a lot, Jean-Paul. Would you like to know about my past relationships? I am very handsome and people are very attracted to me. But, do you know, it's nothing to me, and it is everything to those fools."

"Am I a fool?"

"Yes," and he laughed.

"I know."

"But I want you, Jean-Paul, but only in my own way."

"Then that is enough," I replied. In my mind, Joseph kissed me on the lips. I saw Judas. I saw a vision of Judas looking excitedly at the coupling of Jesus and John. I tasted blood in Joseph's kiss, but it tasted of water, a taste of almost nothing. It was all he could give me and yet I told myself I loved him. I said this over and over again. I would love him and be alone. He would never be truly there.

11

We hunted for a flat, but it was not easy to find a decent flat in Brighton in 1970. Most were degraded with mould, and the walls were nearly always drab, brown and damaged. Tired of the search, I let Joseph hunt alone, and finally he came up with one in Powis Road, whose walls were surprisingly painted black: living room, bedroom, bathroom and toilet. He wanted to touch up the black with an extra coat of paint to cover parts that were faded where pictures had been previously hung.

"We'll find some Art Deco furniture and ornaments," he said.

"You haven't asked whether I like Art Deco," I replied.

"You'll love it, because you love me. And anyway, Art Deco is going at a good price now. I know people in the trade who'll give me a good deal. Just write me out a cheque and leave it up to me."

"I didn't know Art Deco was still in fashion."

"I don't care about fashion. I like black. Black and white, with little colour."

"And what about the rent? Is it reasonable?"

"It's a bit high, but we'll manage. I'll sell a few portraits and I'll make the living room my studio. Now, you must see the balcony."

He parted some dirty curtains, and yes, there was a balcony. It had just enough room to lean over and catch a glimpse of the sea. Then I looked towards Powis Square and its gardens facing us.

"I like the oblique sea view, but the square opposite is full of scattered rubbish and dog shit. Had you noticed?"

He looked out towards the gardens.

"I expect someone cleans it up. I hate it when you are not enthusiastic. I can sense you are not enthusiastic about this flat which was bloody hard to find."

"I am just thinking that this is probably not the right place, Joseph."

He sulked. We had two days to decide on it, and during that time he kept away from me. I was worried and confused and confided in the two men in Dorset Gardens.

"He sounds like a scrounger." Both of them said this at the same time. The inevitable pot of tea was served, and the three of us talked the matter over. I said I thought I was in love with him, and they sighed and looked at each other with the sort of look that said I was a fool. I gulped down my tea, apologised for being tired and went to my room. I brought out the drawings, but nothing could relieve me of the tension I was feeling. I wanted both Jesus and John to stop having sex and to give me some advice instead. In this depressed, delusional state I thought I saw Judas smile. Tension and extreme stress bring out the strangest symptoms, and at one point, I reached the limit of what I could bear. I went out and I bought myself some rope. I wanted out. I wanted to hang myself. It had been Judas's option, so why shouldn't it be mine? I was about to make a noose and find a place to hang myself from when the door opened and Joseph came in.

"What the fuck are you doing? Do you want this flat or not? I have an hour left to decide and the two grannies downstairs were not pleased to see me, and now I see you making a *noose*! Don't be such an hysterical queen."

He slapped me hard across the face.

"Now decide," he shouted.

I heard a commotion downstairs, and Joseph opened the door and yelled at them.

"Go find your graveyards and stop interfering with my lover. You've worked him up to this. Stay in your rooms and shut it!"

"Get out! Get out!" they both yelled back.

"Now you *have* to leave," Joseph said laughing. "Pack your things. You are moving into the flat I found."

I felt totally cold, and it was difficult for me to move my limbs. I felt like a puppet, and yet to my disgust I was accepting to be his puppet. Just pull all the strings, I thought, and drag me there.

I stuffed a wad of pound notes into an envelope that had already been used, and scrawled the word *Sorry* on the outside. Joseph saw the word.

"Sorry? Pathetic! What do you owe those ageing bastards?"

"Kindness," I replied, and as I closed the door of the house in Dorset Gardens, I repeated the word. Once outside, to my surprise, Joseph gave me one of his best smiles and carried my luggage.

"You travel light," he said.

I ignored him, and we walked to the flat. My legs could hardly move, and it was difficult keeping up with Joseph's pace. I felt as if I wanted to be sick. Standing at the end of Powis Road, I waited while Joseph made the final arrangements with the agent and got the keys.

"I've got a surprise for you," he said as we entered the flat. I saw the inevitable. The rooms had been filled with 1920s and 30s furniture; Art Deco lamps and dancing figures of women stared at me from various vantage points. The naked dancers surprised me the most. Some held little lamps, and others were so contorted that they looked as if they had stomach aches. I asked Joseph why there were so many women.

"I'm bisexual," he replied casually.

I looked around the rooms in silence. Every Art Deco detail was ready for us, and he threw himself down on a black and white bedspread.

"Let's fuck," he said.

I ignored this and asked him for my set of keys. He threw them at me.

"I'll go and shop," I said, and I knew there was a certain amount of anger in my voice. "Can I choose the food?"

"Buy a bottle of Champagne, some good steaks and fresh vegetables. You can cook, can't you?"

"I'm sure it won't be up to your standard."

"Well, I can cook." Then he laughed mockingly at me, and his beautiful eyes looked ugly, battling with their conflicted green and brown. At that moment I hated his slim body. "I can read your mind," he said, a smirk on his face.

"And what am I thinking?"

"That you despise loving me. A couple of glasses of excellent, and it must be excellent, champagne, will make you adore me, and we can eat naked. Understood?"

"Won't the dancing ladies mind?"

"Now you sound like a queer bitch! Bring your masculinity back or I'll clout you again. I'm horny and I'm hungry."

The evening went as he planned. I let him fuck me. He came inside of me. I felt nothing. All I did was stare at the black walls.

12

Things got better. Joseph became almost loveable. He hired a car, and we made trips out into the countryside. To my surprise he liked nature.

"It's so deceptive," he said to me during one drive. "Outside like this, I feel I could believe in a gentle god, but then I know this world was created by the devil. The sheep look happy, unaware of slaughter. The happy hawks above us are hovering for their prey. Maybe in your next incarnation you'll come back as a mouse. Think of it, those claws bearing down on you and giving you a very painful oblivion."

"I still feel a sense of joy out here as well," I said.

"Joy? What is that?" and he laughed. "I have never felt or used the word."

He looked up at the Downs as he drove. He was a crazy driver. He could observe the road and the sky, and details of nature all at the same time. On one of our trips, we almost smashed into another car … but to return to this specific journey.

"I know joy," I replied.

"Some night, tell me about it. Put it into the recipe of having sex."

As if in total contradiction to his negative views, he always wanted to stop at out of the way churches. He went into every one of them, buying leaflets and postcards, and reading about their construction and the renovations that had occurred over the years.

"Centuries, centuries ago, they believed!" he whispered.

We were at Coombes church, and he stared with intent at the medieval wall paintings that remained, shadowy and almost indiscernible.

"Men and women thought the world was flat," he said slowly. "They were wrong. They did not know it. And they believed in an old benevolent and sometimes angry man they called God, staring down at them from the vast void beyond the clouds. They were wrong. They did not know it. Happiness was possible then. Amidst the wars and the plagues, happiness was possible. There is no real happiness now. Nothing. Zero."

Then to my astonishment, he knelt and kissed the flagstones. I could hardly believe what I was seeing. I realised I did not understand this man.

"Joseph," I cried out.

Then he lay flat out on the stones and burst into tears, face downwards.

"Why? Why?" he cried out.

It was at that moment that the woman who looked after the church came in. She looked at Joseph and clasped her hands together.

"Oh, welcome!" she said. Joseph remained still. He looked asleep but was more likely in a trance. "Never before have I seen such devotion towards God," she said. "Never before have I witnessed such freedom in action."

Joseph slowly got to his feet, and then turning to the woman, he spat in her face.

That concluded our visits to old churches. I never discovered any motive for Joseph's behaviour towards the woman or why he wanted to prostrate himself. I knew it was useless to try to understand.

In the car that day at Coombes he added mystery to mystery. In a sing-song voice he recited nursery rhymes. Sideways I glanced at his green eye, which was nearest to me, and it looked as glassy as a pool covered in frost. A frozen pool with no water beneath. Dried up. Dead. The green disappearing and replaced by black.

13

Things got worse. In the afternoons he would ask me to remain in the bedroom while he painted in the living room. The canvases were stacked one against another along one of the walls in the living room, and he refused to show me what he had created. All I knew was that he liked to paint portraits of artists from the past, but as he said, they hardly ever sold. I presumed the stacked canvasses were of them. The only time I tried to turn them around, he hit my hands and ordered me to never do it again. I cried out as he had hurt my fingers, and taking me in his arms he pressed his body against mine, I almost suffocated in his embrace, his fierce kisses almost closing off my breath.

"Never do that again," he whispered in my ear.

I struggled and broke free from him.

"Why shouldn't I see them?" I asked.

"They are third rate," he replied.

I said nothing in reply, but left the flat. It was midday. I began to do this almost every day, precisely at twelve, walking the streets of Brighton until six in the evening. I got very tired doing this, and bored at the repetition of it. When I returned, he even thanked me every time for giving him total freedom, and in the evenings, he watched old films on the TV set he had bought with my money. He especially liked black and white films set in the 1930s. He always commented on the accuracy or the inaccuracy of the Art Deco furniture and objects, and had a passion for Ruby Keeler.

"I would love to make love to her if she were here in this room, alive and desiring me," he said while watching one of her films.

I replied coldly, "She *is* alive. You should try to contact her. She would be flattered, and maybe you would be her type."

"Maybe I will," and he clapped his hands together like a pleased child. Then his face turned solemn. "But then, you would be jealous. You would drive her away, Jean-Paul, wouldn't you?"

"On the contrary," I replied.

"So, you wouldn't mind if I went to bed with a woman?"

"Not at all. You told me you were bisexual. You shouldn't deny what must be an important part of you."

He turned off the television in the middle of the film, leant back on the white Art Deco sofa and sighed.

"If I want to go with a woman, I will. At present I don't want to. I suppose it could be interesting if you watched. Somehow I sense more perversity in you than there is in me." He paused, then added, "And you have now ruined my pleasure watching *42nd Street*."

"*You* turned it off. They will show it again."

"Oh, just shut the fuck up," he said angrily.

"This is a trivial row," I replied.

"It goes deeper than you think."

"Oh, and in what way is it deep?"

Shouting out the words, he now launched into a major row.

"You ruin everything! You are a tight-arsed bastard. Do you think I *like* fucking you? Why isn't your arsehole bigger? Why do you clasp my cock so tightly? I like looser arseholes, and you don't have one. Why should I remain faithful to you?"

"Alright," I yelled back. "Go and fuck elsewhere. Just make sure they have money. I may have a tight hole as you crudely put it, but I don't have a tight bank account."

"Are you calling me a whore?"

"Yes."

He leapt off the sofa and hit me harder than he had before. He hit my whole body. I tried to fight back, but he was the stronger. Eventually the battle stopped and wearily he asked me in a casual voice if I wanted a drink.

"Go to Hell," I replied.

"I am in Hell."

"Then stay there."

I went to the bathroom and assessed the damage he had done. I saw how his thick red hands had bruised me and that my face was bruised as well. I looked at myself and thought, this is what they call love. Bruises and traces of blood.

He came into the bathroom.

"I'm sorry," he said.

I turned and stared at him. We stared at each other silently for a while. Then I asked, "Why aren't *you* bleeding? I thought I hit you hard enough. Why do your bruises never show? Does nothing hurt you?"

"I'm sorry," he repeated and came closer to me.

"Back off," I cried out.

Instead of this, he moved slightly forward.

"Back off, Joseph. I mean it."

I picked up a naked razor blade and moved towards him. His face went white with fear.

"Don't cut me," he said.

"I'd like to cut you to shreds with this," and I meant it.

"Not my face, please, not my face. It's all I have. It's all anyone wants from me. My supposedly beautiful face. Don't destroy it."

I moved further forwards and said, "I want to cut deep into you."

He backed away again and screamed, "No!"

I dropped the blade and ran from the bathroom. No, I hadn't cut him, but I had intended to. In the darkness of my soul I wanted to disfigure him for life, and even wash my hands in his blood. That was how profound my love was.

14

The sea was rough. On the beach it leapt at me like a wild dog. My trousers were wet. My face, sprayed with water. I sat on the pebbles, watching and waiting for the next wave. It came, and it attacked again. This was my punishment. I wanted my death, and I wanted the sea to kill me.

"What are you doing?"

I felt my body being dragged away from destruction.

"Don't you know how dangerous this is?" the voice said behind me. "It's one of the roughest nights. I haven't seen a night like this for a long time."

"I want to end it," I cried out, and looking up, I saw an older man's face staring down at me.

"What have you done?" he asked. Then he pulled me to my feet. "I'll drive you home."

His voice was gentle, but it had force enough to combat the elements around us.

"I don't have a home. I've left it," I replied.

The salt in my mouth revolted me.

"Then come back to my place," he said.

Mechanically I responded, "Yes."

"You've had a proper soaking."

The cast iron pillars of the Palace Pier towered above us as he steered me up the beach and onto the lower promenade. When we reached his car, he brought out a blanket from the back and told me to take off my clothes and to cover myself with it.

"Here?" I asked.

"There's no one around. It's fortunate I like storms. I like to walk on stormy nights. Most don't. And now, change. I won't look."

With difficulty, I undressed, but the car was big enough for me to be able to do so. I wrapped the blanket around my body and I felt warmer. He turned and saw that I was finished, then sat down beside me.

"You need a hot drink as well," he said. "By the way, my name is Eric."

He drove the car eastwards, towards his flat in Sussex Square. I felt ridiculous, naked except for the blanket, and I stared automatically at the architecture I was passing. I disliked the chic blackness of Royal Crescent, and was indifferent to the darkened white of the mainly Georgian buildings that followed. Inwardly I laughed at the Corinthian columns and their self-importance; a signal that this part of Brighton was aware of its privilege, and in some ways separate from the rest of the town.

"Do you like it here?" I asked Eric.

"I inherited the flat. My father used to own the whole building. Now Sussex Square is almost all flats, but I call the place I live in, home. The part of it I occupy, used to be my father's extensive library. He needed three rooms for it."

He parked the car and turned to look at me.

"Can you wait in the car while I fetch some clothes for you? We have more or less the same height and figure."

"Suppose somebody passes by the car? That really would be embarrassing."

"Better than being seen naked in the hallway."

Reluctantly, I agreed that as my seat was next to the gardens, I would be more or less in darkness.

He laughed and got out of the car, and I watched as he went into the house. After a few minutes the lights were turned off in the second floor flat. The wind rustled the trees violently beside me, and after what seemed a long time, the outer door opened and Eric placed a pair of trousers, some shoes and a thick green sweater onto my lap.

"To protect your modesty, I will stand outside with my back to the car," he said.

"You don't have to."

"It's okay, I like the wind. Afterall, I did go out to see how rough the waves were."

"And you found me," I replied.

"I am glad," Eric replied, and closed the car door. He then pressed his back against the window, blocking out almost all of the remaining light. With a certain amount of awkwardness, I managed to squeeze into the clothes. I saw the funny side of it and laughed at my own contortions. The sweater was the most difficult and I almost got stuck. It was too tight on me, and I surmised that Eric's torso was thinner than mine. The brown shoes however were too big, and I padded them out with tissues I found in the car.

"I am ready," I shouted.

The wind was racing at almost hurricane speed, and we both ran to the portico of the house. Eric fumbled with the keys, and after what seemed a long while I was in the stuccoed hallway. I stared at its elaborate, glaring whiteness. A man passed us on the stairs and smiled.

Once inside the flat, I looked up at the over-decorated ceiling, then at the walls. Spaced out perfectly, I saw a gallery of paintings. I noticed a Georges Braque and asked Eric if it was a copy.

"Original," he replied. "I share my father's passion for Cubists. There are three Braques and one Gris."

"I like them," I said, and I did. It made a change from the naked canvasses I had lived with in Powis Road.

"Now for food and a hot drink. Tea or coffee? I'm afraid there's no alcohol."

"Coffee please."

"Sit down and relax, and for heaven's sake, take off those dreadful shoes. I'm sorry I forgot socks. I've got some thick ones and I am sure that they will pad you out."

I took off my shoes and saw him glance at my feet for longer than a mere look required. Was he attracted to feet? He seemed to read my mind and scurried out of the room. My toes felt an intrinsic gratitude at being naked, and I wriggled them. In a couple of minutes, he returned with thick white socks. I thanked him and put them on.

"I'll go and rustle up some food and of course, coffee. Black or with milk?"

"Black," I replied.

Alone in the room for a good half an hour, I went over and looked at the paintings. My favourite was one of Braque's. Its intensity of browns and shades of green, with dark orange to one side, appealed to me. *BACH* in bold, black letters, with *J.S.* beneath, startled, and yet startled so well that the name detracted nothing from the rest. A homage of course to the composer. Also, the confusion of planes, with hints of depth, added to the beauty of it all. In silence the whole work rang out its music. A masterpiece of spatial relationships.

"I like its broken-up classicism," Eric said. I was so engrossed, I had not heard him re-enter the room.

"Do you also like Bach?" I asked, still staring at the painting.

"Yes. Would you like me to put some on?"

"Yes, I'd like that."

"Your choice?" he asked.

"*The Goldberg Variations.*"

"Did you by the way notice the violin in the painting?"

I looked again and saw it at once. "You're right!"

"Can I refuse your choice and choose *Concerto for two Violins*?"

"Introduce me to it," I replied.

As we talked, I was excited at the tone of our conversation. It came from another world, far from the one I was used to. Joseph would have hated the surroundings and the music. In fact, he didn't like music at all. Suddenly I felt inwardly that I was in an environment that although foreign, suited me.

"All this pleases me," I said. "Once again, I want to thank you."

We talked for at least two hours more.

15

Eric made no attempt to seduce me. Two days passed, and the storm still raged outside. Inside I felt a grateful comfort and a peace that was new to me. Bach's *Concerto for two violins in D minor* was played often, and as the unspoken affection between us grew it became as it were *our* music. It's complexity, simplicity, and beauty of sound, fulfilled the room and filled the space that was between us. We were united in this music.

"Do you believe in God?" I asked him.

"I know He's not here, and that I will never know Him, but yes. Outside of everything, yes."

"I don't understand."

"Don't try," he said, and smiled at me, a smile that was meant and not faked. It came, I thought, from deep inside of him.

16

Just below the Downs, in the village of Fulking, there is a pub called The Shepherd and Dog, and it was there one evening that Eric took me. I was feeling a weight of unexpected depression, and he thought this place would revive me, or at least that I would enjoy one of the finest places in Sussex. We sat outside the terrace of ancient cottages that made up the pub, and sitting on a long wooden bench with my hands on the equally long wooden table I faced the trees and the upward slope of the Downs. I listened to the gurgling of the stream and some bird with a yellow breast flew down to the water, no doubt to drink, or wash its feathered body.

"Beautiful," I said.

"Yes," Eric replied, and he reached across the table and touched my hands.

"I wish I knew the names of all nature's creatures," I said, "but then, it is impossible to know everything."

"You look pale," Eric murmured. "Why don't we move to the garden below. From there you will get the full evening light, and there is a breeze. We can come here any evening you wish, to get some colour back in your cheeks."

"You take good care of me," I said.

"I am concerned about you."

I smiled at Eric and made the first move to go to the garden, and sitting on similar seats, we heard the quiet chatter of other visitors. Bright though the light was, I felt suddenly as if I was in darkness. Joseph, I thought. It is Joseph.

"What would you like to drink, Jean-Paul?"

"A lager," I replied.

"Not something stronger?"

"It's strong enough for me at the moment," I laughed.

He smiled at me and made his way through one of the doors that led inside.

Turning to one side I saw four youths at the next table to ours. They were talking about exams and how difficult they were to pass. All of them were handsome and one had tawny red hair similar to Joseph. He had his back to me, so could not see me staring at him but an older youth facing him saw my look and whispered in the ear of the youth next to him who was slim and blond. The red-haired boy who was wearing a green sweater, moved forward to hear what they were saying. All four of them had drinks, and each had a bowl filled with chips in front of them. I watched as the redhead slowly dipped a chip into some ketchup and then raised it to his lips. I wanted to be that chip. I wanted to be it, and to follow its path through his digestive system. I wanted to travel to where it would become excreta, ready to be expelled from his system. In this state of dark obsession, I wanted to fall from his anus into the porcelain bowl—the bowl of dirty water. I wanted to be his waste and to die after that brief, or perhaps hours-long time within him.

I felt Eric shaking me.

"What is it? What happened? You passed out!"

We were beside the car, and he opened the door for me to get in.

"One of those youths heard you cry out," he said. "A nice guy. He laid you out on the bench."

"Did he have red hair?" I mumbled, half-conscious, half in the land of nowhere.

"Yes. What about it?"

"It was—" and then I was sitting back in the car.

"It was what?"

"Too red. Far too red and—"

"And? And what, Jean-Paul?"

"I can't remember."

"Well anyway, he heard you call out," Eric continued. "You had fallen to the ground. He thought you were dead. It was then he laid you out on the bench and opened your mouth. He breathed into your mouth, long deep breaths. He was exhausted."

"His lips were on mine?"

"Yes, Jean-Paul, on your lips. What happened to make you pass out like that?"

"It overcame me. It was an assault of disgusting images."

"You have no idea how happy I am that you are fully conscious again."

I fell asleep as the car backed out of its parking space and then turned the bend that led back into the village.

17

I was ill. Eric's doctor called it a total collapse; a fatigue that kept me in bed for many weeks. I'm not sure I even dreamt. It was a kind of coma, and peaceful. I was out of life, and yet, dimly conscious that Eric was nearby. As I slowly got better, I saw that he had made a temporary bed next to mine. The day I felt truly better, he kissed my cheek.

"I am here," he said simply.

I looked at him and then around the room. There was a window open in front of me. I thought I saw a large tree, but it was in fact in my imagination. My first venture out of bed was dizzying, and gently Eric put me back inside the sheets. Once leaning back on cushions, I felt steady, and my sight was clearer. I saw things as they were.

"You must be hungry."

"A little," I replied.

"Agnes who comes in to clean every other day has made you a light broth. She is Scottish, and very proud of it. Will you try a little?"

"Please thank her," and then I added, "I look forward to meeting her."

"She will fuss over you."

And she did, everyday, until I was able to get up and walk around easily, she brought me food and sat by my bed as I ate it. The stronger I was, the more food she fed me. I asked her about her life.

"What is there to say about life, Jean-Paul? It is hard work to live, but it is worth it."

"And your life outside of here?"

"I live in one room. I can't afford more. As I said, it is hard work to live. But I like working for Mr. Eric. I am happy here. The days when I am not working, I sit in the park." She paused, and then added, "When you are ready to go out, perhaps we can meet up. I could make us a packed lunch. Would you like that?"

"Which park do you go to?"

"Queens Park. I like to watch them play tennis. Do you like tennis?"

"I could learn," I said, and she laughed.

"And why not? We should all learn new things in life. I used not to be able to cook very well, but I bought many cookery books and learnt. Now I don't need them. I use my imagination when I make meals. I make mistakes sometimes, but that is part of living too, isn't it?"

"I have made many mistakes, Agnes," I replied.

"Oh, in one's twenties that is normal. Better to make them when you are young than when you are old like me."

"You're not old," I said politely.

She touched my hand gently and whispered, "You should always tell the truth, Mr. Jean-Paul. Look at all the pathways on my face. Every one of them has been a journey. Sixty-eight years of journeys."

"And what has been your best journey?" I asked.

"My marriage. I was young. He was young. Neither of us had journey lines on our faces then. A year after our marriage, he died of pneumonia. It was then I saw just one line on his face. I knew that that one line was his only journey and that he had made it with me. I touched the line with my fingertips on his deathbed. He was dead, but I saw him smile."

"You *actually* saw it?" and I looked into her grey eyes.

"Yes, I saw it. I can never see a smile without thinking of it. He was telling me in that smile that he was happy, and in a happy place. I still feel him watching over me. He was handsome, and he will always be so, wherever that place is after death."

"I'm sorry."

She took the tray from my bed and held it close to my body.

"I am not sorry. I know he is with me."

Eric came in, and no doubt heard the last sentence.

"Agnes, don't tire Jean-Paul." He said quietly.

I came to her defence.

"Agnes and I are going to have a picnic in the park, Eric. We are looking forward to it, aren't we?" and I turned to face her.

"Yes, very much so," she replied.

After she left the room, Eric sat by my bed.

"Has she tired you out?" he asked.

"Not at all. I like her."

"As much as you like me?" he asked teasingly.

"What do you think, Eric?"

"I think you do. I also think we should plan a holiday once you are well."

"Do you know where?" I asked.

"Wherever you like. In this country? Or would you like to go to Paris? As a tourist this time. See it afresh."

I shook my head.

"I'm not ready for that."

"Then what about if I drive you down to Italy? Rome would refresh us both. Might even make you very happy."

"I am content," I replied.

"But that is not the same thing, Jean-Paul. I am assuming you have never been there."

"No, I have never been there."

"I know a good small hotel in Trastevere. From the windows you can see splendid sunsets. During the day I can show you the Pantheon, and we can walk the wonderful streets around it. Nothing is more satisfying than eating a meal in the centre of Rome, and believe me, the happiness of others in the city is contagious. You need a good experience, and the place can show you so much that you will never experience here. I too experienced it when I was your age. I want to give you this gift."

"Thank you," I replied.

"I promise you I will drive well. And we can stop off at so many places on the way. For example, a stopover in Milan. Coffee in the Galleria, and a view of the Cathedral. A cathedral like no other." He paused. "Beauty for us both."

I closed my eyes. I did not want to reply to all this. He kissed me on the cheek, and I heard him cross the room and close the door behind him.

18

Rome was beautiful. How could it be otherwise? We sat side by side in a café on the Piazza di Spagna, near the Spanish Steps. For a while we watched the vivid life around us, and then Eric said, "You have not mentioned it, but are you surprised that during our stay we have always slept in separate rooms?"

I was silent. For some reason I felt afraid. What hidden thoughts and feelings was Eric going to reveal? I felt that something was hanging in the balance. Then he spoke again.

"I would be lying to you if I said I didn't find you attractive, and I do desire you, but more than that, I desire you as a companion. I could spend the rest of my life with you as a companion, and you have no idea how you enrich me. You have made me see this city afresh. You have even taught me things. In the Sistine Chapel, you pointed out figures I had never noticed before. You made me aware of Michelangelo's genius, and truthfully, I doubted it before."

"I read my books and I look at closeups of places and works of art. It is just my reading and seeing that I have given you. You see, Eric, I did not want you to find me ignorant about what I would see here. I wanted to give you as much information as I could to show you that I knew about all these things. You could consider me a fake."

Eric smiled at this and said nothing. I glanced at the rising steps, so rich in living, and knowing how to live. Then I faced Eric and smiled.

"Truly I feel at peace with you."

"Thank you," Eric replied. "Now, shall we walk through the Villa Borghese Gardens? And then make our way to the Via Veneto?"

"I have a feeling you want to tell me something," I said.

"For the moment I think I have said enough. We will talk more later, while we have another drink. Do you know, Claudia Cardinale used to drink at the Via Veneto. I was told that years ago. I never saw her then. Why is it that we idolise those gods and goddesses of the cinema? It's a mystery to me. Seeing *her* on the screen, she totally enchants me. Not sexually of course, but as someone to have dinner with. I would say *yes* immediately. Do you remember her in Visconti's *The Leopard?*" and he looked around him. "I am talking about trivialities, but inside I am trembling." He then looked at me and our feelings connected. "You too are afraid, aren't you?"

"I was a few minutes ago, I don't want to lose you, Eric."

"Agnes talks about the travel lines on her face. Do you see mine? I'm almost an old man, and inside of me I feel older still. And yet with you, and you alone, I feel otherwise. How complex we humans are."

I looked at Eric and saw a good-looking man. In Paris I had always been with men of my own generation. With Eric, I had crossed over the barrier of youth. I would have slept with him, had sex with him if he had wanted me. Love is a broken word, but I loved him.

"Smile at me," Eric asked.

I reached out and entwined his fingers with mine. It was my left hand and with my right I pointed out the view in front of us.

"Come on!" I said. "Let us make our way to the place of the gods and goddesses. I too would see Claudia Cardinale in anything."

Relaxed by my exaggerated words, he replied, "Yes, but I expect they are up there in the clouds. In homes made by our dreams."

We both laughed and made our way towards the Piazza del Popolo.

19

The Via Veneto was lined with chairs and tables, and the place was packed, but Eric commented how there was *nobody* there to see, look at, or dream about. He looked like an aged child who had had his toys smashed. I tried to make a joke of it and told him to look up into the sky. Night had almost fallen, and he peered up at the dimming of the light, and said, "What do you see?"

"They're all there," I whispered, "all waiting to appear. The stars are ready to shine and to smile at us. The gods and goddesses of the cinema are just waiting for people to leave so we can be alone with them. Imagine it, Eric. Make it real in your mind."

He sighed and sat down at one of the few spare tables. I joined him.

"I am sorry, Jean-Paul. You see, I am far too young, and at the same time, far too old. And now, I must say what I have to say." He paused for a while, then drew in a deep breath as if he was about to plunge into hidden depths. "You see, I was with *him* the last time I was here. About *him*. There is always an essential *him* in our past, isn't there? Unlike you, he was not handsome. The skin on his face and back were disfigured with acne. But his eyes! I fell in love with his eyes. His dark, beautiful eyes. The way he looked intently at everything. At me, at others, and his look always told the truth. He saw *into* others, and he saw into me and himself. He saw too the faultline, and that faultline was that he could not reciprocate what I felt for him. We flew to Rome. We shared the same bed. He gave me his body, and as I touched him, I knew he loathed the touch. Once I scratched his back during sex and opened some of the sores. Pus and blood were on my hands, and still I loved him. I will always love him."

Then Eric was silent.

"You perhaps wish he was here instead of me?" I asked.

"Oh no, no. You give me so much else. I want to live with you. Give you a good life. I love you differently, but I know at the core of my being, *he* will always shadow me. And as I sit here now on the Via Veneto, I see him and yet I only want to see you. Is life all one long contradiction?"

"Yes, Eric, I believe it is. In fact, you want him *and* me to be beside you now. Isn't that how you feel?"

"Yes. I want you to help me make that possible."

A waiter interrupted us, and Eric ordered two vodkas, assuming that I wanted vodka as well, and as the waiter walked away, he called out, "And a finger bowl."

From the inside of the café, I could hear popular music. My Italian was just good enough to realise that the woman was singing about the loss of love.

"How do you want me to help?" I asked.

"Can we walk a little?"

"But you've just ordered!" I paused, then said, "I want you to explain here and now, in what way I can do something for you. After all, you have done so much for me. Don't be afraid of being completely honest about your needs."

Time was passing, and lights were turned on. The crowd on the street intensified, and I realised the Via Veneto was at its peak. Women lavishly dressed and made-up, men in tailored suits, and a few gay men flamboyantly throwing kisses to each other across separate tables. The women laughed loudly, and the men responded loudly. I felt a lightness in my stomach as if some inner weight were being lifted and I felt a floating feeling that I am not sure I had ever experienced before. I felt joy, and anything Eric wanted from me, I would give him. I touched his hands again, and again his fingers entwined with mine. For those who were looking, they must have thought we were lovers, and in a way we were. In my groin, my penis stirred, but it was not for Eric. It was for desire itself. If he had asked me then to have sex with him, I would have agreed.

"Whatever you want, Eric, I will give you. I know you say you don't want it, but could my body satisfy you just once?"

"It wouldn't work between us. And that is no insult to you. You are for a man of your own age or even younger, and if Ben could see you now, he would really want you."

"Is Ben his name?"

"Yes."

I tried to guess ahead about other things, but failed. The noise around us was full of voices; Italian mostly, but a forest of other languages also. Rome was a tower of Babel, and the floating feeling intensified, lifting me above the crowd. I saw myself in a bubble above the long line of chairs and tables, and I had the capacity to understand all of the mingled languages. And among this crowd there was one word above all others that I heard the most: desire. A vast desire, not only for bodies, but for the city itself; its slums and its variegated places of beauty. Rome in all its gaudy splendour, where rich men bought and sold, where prostitutes of both sexes dressed as people of virtue and gay youths danced into the arms of film stars. And I thought of all those Hollywood stars sinking to their knees in hotel corridors, caressing the genitals hidden beneath willing clothes. And so many were willing, from the poor who flooded the centre of Rome, greedy for money offered, to the waiters in the best hotels who serviced both men and women, and the elderly women who opened up their wrinkled arms to those who despised them. Rome was the capital of all this; baroque and beautiful, petrified in its history and its history to come.

Eric was shaking me.

"You are in a trance," he said.

"Of joy."

"To be here?"

"Yes, a thousand times yes."

"And could you be here with Ben?"

The question had now been directly asked.

"Of course, of course," and the inner floating which had gone outwards, shrank inside of me. The bubble burst. The crowd had dispersed.

"Don't say it so easily," Eric replied.

"Everything is easy if it is done without shame."

Eric sat for a while in silence, and under the artificial light his eyes fixed themselves on me. Eventually he spoke.

"Could I ring him and invite him to visit us here? His fear of seeing others is great. He just stays in his London flat, and dreams of being loved, and hates himself for seeing it as an impossible dream."

"And you want me to make the dream come true? Suppose he doesn't like me, respond to my looks."

"He'll find you as handsome as I find you handsome. I am sure of that. And with persuasion on your side, he would open his arms and free himself of self-loathing."

I leant back in my chair. The waiter was hovering.

"I'd like another vodka," I said to him, then added, "make it two."

The vodka came and I felt very clear in my mind. If the young man was passable, I would give him what he needed. Not love, but its counterfeit; which very often appears as real.

"Can you describe Ben more to me? I want every detail."

"He is the same height as you, with reddish to light-brown hair and dark, dark eyes."

"That *does* excite me," I added.

"His body is slim, and his flesh taut. He eats very little, fearing that food will worsen his acne. It can be a terrible affliction, you know. Of course we can all get the occasional spot, and even with just one we do our best to get rid of it. You are fortunate in having a perfectly clear skin, but imagine if you can, pustules on your nose, on the corner of your mouth. A row of them on your forehead, and some so big on the cheeks of your face that you want to destroy yourself."

"I can imagine it," I said.

"I don't think you can. In Paris, did you ever go with a boy or a man looking like that?"

I shook my head in silence.

"And none of your lovers ever developed any signs of it happening?"

"A spot occasionally, yes, but nothing like you describe."

"Then you do *not* understand how Ben feels."

"I have my imagination. I've seen people with severe acne on the street."

"Young men?"

"Yes."

"And inside yourself, you rejected them at once."

"I suppose you could say that."

We both paused, and more vodka was ordered. As the waiter took his time to bring the drinks, I began to wonder if I could go along with this need of Eric's. Then the vodka arrived, and fortified by it, I was determined to try to satisfy Ben.

"Jean-Paul, do you think you will be able to get an erection and sustain it?"

"There are ways," I replied.

"Such as?"

"By concentrating my mind on Joseph, and also on Ben's hair, which you say is reddish. I can stare at it as we caress, as we—"

"—fuck?" Eric concluded.

"Is he passive or active? I am both."

"Mainly passive."

"Then I would have sex with him while he lies face down. I would easily keep my erection."

For a while again there was silence between us.

"What does Ben do? What is his job?"

"He works at home, for a newspaper. Politics. The theory of it more than anything. He is never asked to meet people or to go to countries with political problems or wars."

"The editors must like him."

"There is nothing to dislike in Ben as a person."

"And here in Rome? You really want him to come here again

where the physical self is such a priority? The body here is everything."

"It would be a challenge. It was before, but he came."

"And will you tell him the reason why he is needed here?"

"Of course not. Remember, I am still in love with him. The tragedy of this, if you can call it that, is that I never found any fault in his looks. I was the perfect lover, but I was not perfect enough for him."

"You are a good man," I whispered.

"Call it what you like, but he was—is—?" and I could see tears in Eric's eyes.

"Won't it be hard on you, seeing me, whom you also love but in a different way, making my attempts to seduce him, to make him feel desired emotionally and physically?"

"You are the only person I can ask to do this, precisely because I love you. I will feel happy that he is happy with you."

I got up and looked at Eric.

"Can you wait for me here? I feel so much inside of me. I am overwhelmed. A love like you feel for him could break any heart. I have never heard such an expression of devotion, or consistency in loving. *Never*!" I concluded emphatically.

"Go for a walk, Jean-Paul, but can I ring him?"

"Tonight?"

"Tonight."

"Yes. Ring him. Make sure that you do," and I smiled at Eric.

I decided to walk in the Villa Borghese Gardens, and I sat there for a long time. Could I do it? I asked myself. The question reverberated inside of me. Then I understood that I had to act out of my feelings towards Eric. I did not think of the word love, but of need, and the need of giving myself to Ben was clearly essential to all of us. I made my way back to the Via Veneto.

20

"Ben is arriving today. He didn't hesitate for a second."

"He still loves you," I said.

Eric sighed.

"We are meeting up in a café, just him and me, near the Pantheon."

We were having a drink at the time. Eric had opened a bottle of wine, but for some reason I automatically raised the glass to my lips and tasted the remnants of wine at the bottom. I examined the red stain that remained. Would I too be stained by this desire of Eric's to try to make Ben happy, sexually and emotionally? The red stain somehow seemed like a warning. I wondered how I could satisfy this young man. What if I was not attracted to him? And if I was, would he accept my embraces, and would they give him some level of fulfilment?

"I have worked it all out," Eric said. "It may sound ridiculous, but I have found a way for you to meet him accidentally. I have made a reservation for you in the same hotel he will be staying in. You will be there for several days. After say the second or third day, you will meet accidentally outside his room. You will pretend to be drunk and you will try to enter his room by mistake. You will make a lot of noise. He will be in the room and be surprised by the sound. He will open the door, and you will collapse against him."

"It sounds like a Feydeau farce," I replied. "I won't actually be drunk. Surely he will know I am acting. Don't you see how farcical this is, Eric? It is a ridiculous plan."

We were silent for a while until Eric broke the silence.

"I know you can do it. Just muss your hair up and look a bit dodgy on your feet. He won't have time to smell your breath as you fall against him. And kind as I know he is, he will take you into his room. After that he will make you coffee and you will act as if you are slowly feeling better."

"Beautifully put, Eric."

"I see no other way, Jean-Paul. I want you both to begin to make a connection. I know there are possible alternative ways, but he is very intelligent and if I for example introduced you to him as a friend, he would be immediately suspicious. I tried this once before and it was a total failure. The meeting between you must happen in a way that is as I have said, accidental. And the intimacy of a hotel room gives an opportunity for total privacy."

I poured myself another glass of wine and with a certain irony in my voice I said to Eric, "Maybe I should get completely drunk now. We could act it out and see if you think it works. Unfortunately, I still find this rather ridiculous."

"What are you really feeling, Jean-Paul?"

I laughed as I put the glass of wine down on the table. Then I risked all and said something I realised might hurt him.

"Eric, when you saved me on the beach and took me back to your place, were you already thinking of this? I don't want to think this, but I can't help but wonder if you already saw me as available for such a plan."

"I don't know how many times I have to tell you that I love you. I'm not *in* love with you, but I love you enough to want you with me and in my life for the rest of my remaining life. You must never, never doubt this. It is true that I am still *in love* with Ben, and strange though it may sound, it would make me happy to see you together. And of course, to be with you together, but not all of the time. I also think that if this works out between you, happiness will come from it."

"In my way I love you too, Eric. I still find this planned meeting absurd, but I will do my best. You mentioned the word happiness. What if I am not totally happy with him?"

Eric poured himself a glass of wine and sipped from it.

"If you need other lovers than Ben, then you will have to

have them. And if everything falls apart, I am here for you both, with love and no reproaches. That I assure you."

He put down his glass and said with a sadness in his voice, "Either this will be a nightmare or it will be a dream come true, but I know neither of us can predict what will happen or what either of you will feel."

21

Clumsily I fell against Ben's door. I was totally sober, had put on my worst clothes and mussed up my hair to give a not very flattering view of myself. I had in fact made myself look a wreck. At first there was no sound, so I fell again, very heavily this time, against the solid brown door and sang out very loudly a Francoise Hardy song: *L'amour d'un garcon*. I thought it appropriate and just hoped that he understood a little French. Then the door opened, and I slumped onto the soft carpet that all first-class hotel rooms have. Ben closed the door. I was inside.

"Sorry," I said, and my eyes were closed.

"Are you ill?" and I heard his voice. It was soft and gentle, and I liked it. He was bending over me, and I half opened my eyes. Ben appeared young and slim, and his face was not as scarred as I had expected.

"Sorry," I repeated. "Wrong room."

"I'll help you up."

His arms were strong, and I felt them close around my torso and with a little effort of my own I was on my feet. I actually did feel giddy. Perhaps it was the excitement of all that was happening. My heart was beating very fast.

"There's a sofa here. Sit down on it."

"Thank you. Very kind. I'm Jean-Paul."

"I'm Ben. It's not exactly the time to say I'm pleased to meet you, but then a sudden visit like this is well—exceptional, isn't it?"

"Had too much to drink," I mumbled. "A night on the tiles. Stupid of me. Too many straight vodkas."

I lay out on the sofa and Ben drew up a chair and looked me

over. The giddiness had subsided, and I stared at him. Yes, the acne was there, and yes, there was one on his nose.

"I must look a mess," I said.

"You don't look so bad. Just lie there, and I'll make some coffee. Only instant, but it will perhaps help." He got up and I watched his back as he moved away from me. The sweater he was wearing was tight and I liked his shape and very visible broad shoulders. His buttocks were tight and small, and I imagined him naked, which gave me an erection. I felt happy at this first reaction. Still with his back to me he asked, "Would you like some sugar in it?"

"No, black," I replied.

He took a little longer than he should have, and I supposed he was aware of his skin and too alarmed by my presence to show it to me more than he had to.

"The kettle is slow," he said. "In a good hotel you would think they would have faster kettles. It is 1970 after all."

"Rome is very ancient," I replied. "They do things differently here."

I heard his laugh, as soft as his voice. I wanted him.

Eventually he turned around and brought over the coffee. He moved the chair and sat behind me and with a sudden and unexpected movement, I turned around and faced him.

"I feel better already," I said, and I saw what I had expected to see. As I had turned, he had momentarily put up his hand to his face. Then he self-consciously let the hand drop.

"It's very nice of you helping me like this. Letting a drunken slob into your room. I really *do* have a room in this hotel."

"Which floor," he asked.

"The one below. Just look at me! Something out of a dustbin. When I went out tonight, I just didn't care what I was wearing. I was in that sort of mood. Do you know what I mean? Do you ever feel like that?"

"You are—" and he did not finish the sentence.

"—a drunken idiot. I went to a bar nearby. Felt lonely. So lonely I did not even bother what people would think of me. I just wallowed in my pitiful state. Loneliness can make you do some very strange things."

"I know what you mean. I don't go out much either." He paused, then added, "Do you like Rome? It's my second visit. I came over to meet a friend. I'm not a tourist."

How long would it be before he knew this ridiculous encounter was concocted by Eric? I wanted to tell him the truth at once, but knew that I couldn't. I realised too that Eric would easily get out of the situation. He would put it down to fate and laugh it off. But then again, wouldn't Ben wonder why he was asked over to see Eric when he was clearly in a relationship with me? I decided on another explanation.

"You may not have noticed me, but I saw you arrive. To be honest, I wanted to get to know you. I thought, I'd really like to be his friend. This may all sound very silly. I wasn't drunk, you see. I made up this terrible bit of theatre to draw your attention to me."

"Wanting to meet me? Why?"

"I told you, I liked you the moment I saw you. I admit that I'm gay. I don't presume that you are, but I still want you as a new friend."

"Oh, I see!" he replied. Then he smiled. "As it happens, I am gay. But putting that to one side, you must have seen me from a distance."

"No. Close-up. I suppose I was just someone in the crowd to you. Please forgive me for being pushy."

"I am flattered. I find it kind of cute that you went to all this trouble to get to know me. I mean, for a start, most people think I'm straight."

"Most people think that *I'm* straight." I paused and laughed. "All this has been some very bad theatre, hasn't it?"

"Yes, it has, but it has amused me."

"I really should apologise."

"No, no, not at all. You are a very good-looking man yourself."

"You too," I said, and then there was a very long silence.

I sat there on the sofa and suddenly felt very angry with Eric. Ben broke the silence.

"Now for some reality. I was told once by someone I really liked that he pitied the fact that I had a pock-marked face. He said it was like making love to a cripple. I never got over the hurt I felt. He got me by telling me that he loved me, and after that he dominated me. In fact, I was just a good fuck, and he dressed that crude fact up with words so emotionally banal I won't bother to repeat them."

I made the lame reply of saying that I thought this was terrible. Inside I was surprised he was so honest so quickly.

"Let's just say, Jean-Paul, I am wary now. Very wary."

"I don't know how to respond to what you have told me." I meant it. I knew perfectly well that men could act cruelly to each other.

He came over and stood in front of me.

"Would you like to count how many spots I have on my face? Do you dare to?"

I felt a terrible sense of shame.

"It's skin deep," I said. "I see a few, but they are part of your face. Your eyes are perfect, your smile, your voice. I heard your voice at the desk when you arrived, and I saw your eyes. For me, the voice and the eyes are the most important."

He stared down at me and said nothing. We remained in silence for what seemed a very long time and neither of us moved. Then he said these terrible words.

"Acne, Jean-Paul, acne make you a monster in our world. Most young men want as near to perfection as they can get, and I am far from being perfect in their eyes. They used me. But then I found out that older men are different. They make compromises, but I'm not physically attracted to them. I can't help it if I'm not. I *have* tried." He paused again and I thought of Eric.

"Can I kiss you?" I asked.

"There is a spot on my lower lip."

"I want you as you are. Is there any way I can prove this to you?"

"Not yet, no you can't. this is all too sudden, too rushed. I don't believe in sudden wanting. I have to trust, and I have very little left of trust in me to do that. But yes, I find you very attractive."

"Then let me just hold you."

There was open hostility in his voice as he cried out, "There are *others*. Many others. You know nothing about me as a person. You say you want me, and yes, I want you as well. Your skin is clear, and your body is just right. But for fuck's sake I am damaged."

"Can we go out tonight at this late hour? A walk through Rome. I won't make any approaches. I promise."

He looked down at the floor.

"I'll meet you in the foyer in half an hour. Perhaps we can find a late-night place to have another drink. I'm inviting you. You see, given the chance, I'm really quite dominant. I like making the decisions. But to be clear with you, I'm not a very nice guy. I work at home in London, a pitiful job as an occasional writer for a newspaper that tells mostly lies. It's easy work but they pay me badly. And I love money. Basically, I'm not that romantic. You have been warned."

"Sometimes one can be romantic despite oneself," I replied.

He changed the subject.

"Your name is Jean-Paul. That's a nice combination of two names. Are you French?"

"Half. My English happens to be better than my French."

"Well," he said, "we know a little bit more about each other."

22

We found a restaurant that was open until three in the morning. Neither of us had eaten since lunch, so we were pleased to find it. We said very little. Ben had a steak, medium, and we chose a good wine. I had pasta, but I was more hungry for Ben than for the food. The cost of the meal was outrageously high, and I had only just enough to pay. Outside, dawn was breaking.

Slowly we walked through Rome, and between the Castel Sant'Angelo and the Vatican I told him the truth. I told him that I was with Eric as a loving companion, but that Eric still loved him and wanted him to be happy with a younger man.

He sighed and then smiled. "So, this was all a set-up. Clever. He *must* love me very much."

"Can you forgive us?" I asked.

"Yes. But what if after seeing me up close, you had felt disgust? How do I know you don't?"

I pushed him gently up against the Vatican colonnade and kissed him. He tried to fight me off at first, then he kissed me back.

"I hope this isn't going to be some kind of threesome," he said.

"It isn't that at all. I love Eric in a very different way. It is not at all physical. Believe me."

Then Ben kissed *me* and pushed his tongue into my mouth. He stepped back.

"Just *want* me physically," he said. "I will know if your body is lying. And even if it is some sort of threesome, so be it. I need Eric as well. In my own way. He has always been generous to me."

23

How futile it was in the end, but I fantasized too much and believed I had fallen in love with him. He went along with my passion, but was remote at the same time. One night after sex I imagined a sort of impossible eternity with him. I would fill him with so much love that he would reciprocate. Since time began, lovers have used that word *eternal*, as if it was an endless road of years that was not finite but infinite, and that the fresh green of youth would never darken. The April of passion would remain always April. I pushed back memories of Joseph. How I deceived myself, and willingly. Real love supposedly replaced by another loving, never believing it was the same deception. In fact, it was desire pushed to the limit. My crime was being adolescent in my feelings. I needed more wisdom to know what a lifetime of fidelity meant.

Then, one day he told me about his past. How he had lived with a mother who beat him often and fed him with reluctance. He was constantly hungry, eating chocolate bars to excess and stealing money from her purse to do so. The meals at his school made him feel ill as the meat and meagre vegetables were often badly cooked and served up nearly cold. He vomited often. He never knew why she had killed herself by putting her head in the gas oven, but he was not sorry. He was put into the hands of relations who had little affection for him. Then the acne began. A breakout at puberty, and other children avoided him. A childhood and adolescence with no love or understanding. He wanted to die, and yet he wanted to live.

He was approached by older men, two of them in their seventies. It was easy to get money out of them. One of them was sadistic and made him wear a surgical mask. The *why* of it, again, he did not know. He was fucked often and hated it. He learnt hatred easily, and yet the men were useful. He always had sex with a T-shirt on, and as he grew older, he continued having sex with his T-shirt on. He did not want anyone to see his back. He was in and out of work, despite the fact he had done well at school. He was greedy for money and lots of it.

It was when he met Eric that he began to change in many ways. He cared for Eric, because he was not disgusted by his body and his face. And although he still did not enjoy going with older men, he attached himself to him. He knew Eric was deeply in love, and that in his own way he was hurting as well.

"Sex stopped," he said. "And we kept in contact. He gave me a monthly allowance. I accepted it. And then you entered his life."

"I have told you; it is platonic, not sexual. It has been like that from the start, Ben."

"Poor Eric! He loves us both, but in my case he fell *into* love, body and soul. I could not bear it, but I forced myself to bear it. As I said, I'm greedy and I needed the money. But believe it or not, I am still in my way, faithful to him. When he needs me, I am there."

Eric lengthened our stay in Rome by two weeks. He gave Ben a sum of money to ensure that he would have sufficient funds, and in the main, Ben paid for most things, and I passively accepted. I was aware that this was, in a sense, a form of prostitution. Eric avoided us, going his own way in Rome, but one night he saw me alone in the Piazza Navona, and came to sit at my table.

"Where's Ben?" he asked.

"His acne has got worse," I replied. "He doesn't want to be out in public, and I could not stand the claustrophobia of the hotel room any longer. He has stopped washing. The room smells. He hates himself."

"But he loves you. He *is* in love with you, isn't he?"

"Oh, Eric. Those words. I am passionate about him, and he

is passionate when he wants to be. Otherwise, we just go through the motions. You see, I still think about Joseph. I am ashamed to say that in Ben's arms, I have started to imagine I am with Joseph, and that I have returned to him. I feel like a criminal. I am still in love with that bastard, and yet my desire for Ben is strong."

"Does he know about Joseph?"

"No,"

"Do you talk at all about your past with Ben?"

"Only in the vaguest of terms. He is acutely sensitive. He does not know that I have had mental collapses. We are both—" and I stopped myself from saying the word.

"You are both what, Jean-Paul?"

"We are both—damaged."

Eric sighed. The additional two weeks were almost over.

"It is time I re-entered your lives actively," he said. "I am strong enough to hold you both. I can see both of you are unfit for work. We will return to England. Yes, that is the right thing to do."

Then in a pleading voice, Eric said to me, "Fall in love with him! I know you can. Reject your memories of Joseph. You feel passion towards him. Passion is the most vital first step to a long-lasting sexual and emotional relationship. I call it being in love. Fall in love with him."

"Yes," I said, to stop the conversation.

24

Once back in Brighton, Eric put up the money for us to rent a flat. It was on Montpelier Road, and it had two bedrooms, a living room, and a bathroom. It had mould in the corners of two of the rooms, but the landlord let it out at an affordable price because he did not want to be reported.

Ben's face broke out with more spots than ever before, and he would not have sex with me, or seek out medical treatment. Eric could do nothing to persuade him and even said he would pay for any doctors' bills, adding that he knew of a good private one.

"Accept Eric's offer," I said to Ben. But his loathing of himself was now too powerful. He was far too pessimistic about his condition and felt that it would never go away even with the best of a doctor's help. He shut himself away in one of the bedrooms and I heard him sobbing every night.

Eric was a calming force, and I spent a lot of my time with him. I told him I wanted to find a steady job, and he found me one in an accountant's office. He was friends with the man who ran the place, and because of that I was paid well. I was good at my job and discovered that I had what they call a mathematical mind.

This was all going well for me. Sexually I found release looking at my images of Jesus, John and Judas. I masturbated enough, usually before going to sleep, and I put earplugs in my ears to shut out Ben's sobbing. I was not being callous. I had a responsibility to look after him as best as I could and had the force of will not to seek sexual satisfaction from him by any sort of force.

It was 1971, and two days into January I found a dusty

painting in a second-hand shop that did not have the status of an antique shop. I showed it to Eric, and he became excited.

"How much do they want for it?" he asked.

"Next to nothing."

"Then give them next to nothing."

The two men who ran the shop knew nothing about art and told us it had come from an elderly Dutch woman who was dying of cancer.

"It's a meaningless daub," one of them said and burst out laughing.

"That's why I like it," Eric replied.

Once back in Eric's flat, he gently dusted off the excessive dirt on the canvas. It was not large, and after his expert cleaning he asked me if I really liked it.

"Yes, otherwise I would not have pointed it out to you."

"It's a school of art called Cobra. I will get it evaluated."

The painting was a depiction of a giant bird, which looked weirdly alive in a blaze or distorted reds and yellows.

"It may be worth a lot." Eric smiled at me as he said this. "Tomorrow I will contact a dealer friend who works at one of the London auction houses. Would you miss it if it went under the hammer for a higher price?"

"You're kidding me," I said.

"No, I'm serious. And to change the subject, make Ben have sex with you. I know he is keeping you at a cruel distance. He has got to grow up and I am sick of hearing about his acne and his need for total seclusion. One day he will have to face the world, and work. He also has to accept that he will grow old, and that when he is old he will need money. Old age is no fun without it. And now to get onto something that I consider important. He won't accept a doctor's help, so perhaps nature will do it for him. He must get some sun on his face. Sun helps, or so I'm told. So, I insist you both have another long holiday, and I will talk to your employer. Adam is a decent guy. He'll keep you on, if I ask him."

I kissed Eric on the cheek.

"You *really* care about us, don't you?"

Eric opened his arms wide and hugged me. "What else do I have in life except you two? I love you both in different ways, but in the end, love is love. You'll find that out one day in the distant future. If you live until you are ninety, which you might, you will look back at your life and see that, despite all the ills that have affected you, life was good—quite simply that. Good."

I walked back to Montpelier Road and found Ben in the living room. He was wearing a surgical mask, a T-shirt and no underwear. He had an erection and was playing with himself. Without saying a word, I went over to him and took his cock into my mouth. I excited him so much he tore off the mask, but not the T-shirt. Panting for breath he cried out, "I want you. I want you." I lifted his legs onto my shoulders and fucked him, and this was the first time he let me do it. I stared at his face and listened to every frantic gasp he made. I shot inside of him and then kissed every spot on his face. I even ripped off his T-shirt and kissed his chest and his back.

"I am your lover," I said. "Accept it."

"You shouldn't have kissed my chest and my back," he replied. "And you shouldn't have kissed the spots on my face. What are you trying to prove?"

I slapped his face, and he looked shocked and frightened.

"Shut up, Ben. You are in love with me. Now say it."

"I am involved with you."

"You are in love with me. And this nonsense about your acne has to end. I will move heaven and earth to make you respect your own body."

"I can't."

"You can and you will." I hit him again, harder than the first time.

"That hurt! Why do you have to be so fucking strong?"

"I have to knock some sense into you. I have to knock out the feelings you have about your blasted acne. And remember, Ben, that I am *not* the passive bastard you thought I might be.

And also listen to this. I was with Eric a while ago, and he reminded me that both of us will grow old. Will your spots matter then? Will anything really matter then? I think something will. And that is loving. Nothing else will matter, only love and the prospect of death. We are born alone, and despite the fact that we are together, we will die alone. How do you think it will feel going out of this world with screams of regret?"

I watched as he covered his face with his hands. The sobbing began again.

"Stop that! One more thing. We will sleep together from now on. Understood?"

His hands fell to his sides and staring at me he murmured, "You have won."

"No one wins, Ben."

Still sexually excited, I fucked him again, and this second time, the orgasm was so fierce that I bit into his neck. Afterwards, I stared down at him and said, "Remember, Ben, it was by Eric's arrangement that you came to me. I won you then. Like a man emerging from a big slot machine, I accepted the gift. I desire you. And I want you. Don't forget it."

25

At auction the painting went for a lot of money, but not quite as much as Eric had expected. He handed it all to me.

"This is for the extended holiday. Now, go somewhere hot if you can, and make Ben *happy*. I love him despite myself. Loving despite oneself is a lonely place to be when you know that the person you love will never, ever be held again in your arms. It's a cold feeling with a volcano beneath."

"I love you," I said.

"To be precise, you love me, but you are not in love with me. Now, with all the cards on the table, I want you both to at least try to find happiness."

His voice trembled and he turned away from me.

"Eric?" I reached out and held his hand.

"I'm just an old fool crying." He turned and faced me. "The absurdity of it! Shouldn't old guys' tear ducts dry up like their sperm does?" Then he laughed. "Self-pity is such a wonderful indulgence."

Ben entered the room, almost as if he smelt the money.

"Impatient, Ben?" Eric asked. And I looked at them both. An invisible flow of bitterness seemed to pass between them. Bitterness and even hatred can often bloom when passion is not reciprocated, whatever Eric would say to the contrary. I sensed the longing Eric felt to kiss those blemishes on Ben's face, and I saw in my mind his fingers breaking open one of the more insistent sores. A futile gesture to show the bitterness of his love.

"The painting sold reasonably well," I said, trying to break any further uneasy moments between them.

"How much exactly?" Ben asked. And that question seemed

crude.

"That's enough from you," I said.

Eric looked at me and murmured, "Show him how much, Jean-Paul."

I placed the wad of notes on the living room table and slowly Ben counted them. He smiled, as the notes got higher and higher. Eric had withdrawn to another part of the room.

"It's for us to go away on holiday," I said. "Say thank you to Eric for making this possible. And to add to that, he has even got me time off from work."

Ben looked over to Eric, and said without a trace of emotion, "Thank you very much for what you have done."

Eric forced a smile and replied, "The sun will do you good, somewhere."

"And I leave the choice of where to go to you," I added. And Ben reached out and touched the pile of notes.

"I'd like to go back to Rome," he said.

On hearing this, Eric left the room, and I heard the flat door close behind him.

"What about Sicily? It's hotter there."

"Tempting, but I would like to spend more time in Rome. You *did* ask me to choose."

I moved close to him, and momentarily he backed away. We were alone and I needed to kiss him, if not on the face then on his slender neck. I wanted to bite him there. I caught at the jacket he was wearing and drew him to me.

"I want you," I said, and bent to reach his neck. Violently he thrust me away.

"No," he cried out. "Not there! There is one of the biggest of *them* there."

For a second or two I found his response comical.

"I don't care about that," I said as gently as I could.

"I do."

"*Them*. What is *them*, Eric? It is superficial. It is something that will go. And it will go. Am I to fight all the time to make love to every part of you?"

He screamed at me, and shouted, "Don't be so fucking positive about all this! I can't bear it, and you don't understand it."

Then he picked up the pile of notes and threw them in my direction. The money scattered all over the carpet, and without replying I picked up each note carefully and after a while put the notes in my trouser pocket.

"Calm down," I said slowly.

"Yes, alright," he snapped back.

"Promise?"

"I told you, yes" and there was a petulant note in his voice.

"Our relationship mustn't be spoilt," I said.

"Rome will cure me. Rome must cure me. If you give me some of the money I will visit a good dermatologist there. I know of one already."

I was surprised at this.

"So that is why you want to return to Rome?"

"I have this intuition that the man I refer to will cure me."

I nodded my head and wondered who this supposedly good dermatologist was. Was it someone we had met? Was it someone *he* had met during our last stay. I took the notes out of my pocket and counted out half of it for him.

"If you want more, tell me," I said. "Now, all we have to do is make the arrangements. And wouldn't it be polite to visit Eric and show him a little bit more affection?"

"I suppose I must, if you think so."

The casual reluctance in his voice sickened me. I felt a sharp pain in my stomach.

26

By day and by night, I saw Ben differently. During the day as we walked through the streets of Rome, I looked at his face and saw how his skin was improving. There were far fewer spots than before and the ones that were there were much smaller, and only the worst of the acne scars showed.

"You look beautiful," I said to him one afternoon while we were inside the Pantheon.

And he replied, "Thank you."

There was heat in the air and his voice was cold.

We had rented a small flat near the Piazza del Popolo, but we were only there for breakfast and to sleep. It belonged to an elderly gay man who had gone into exile in Turkey, and because of that, the flat was always up for rent, and the money sent to a bank in Istanbul. It was through Eric that we found it. Rumour had it the man had committed a crime, but what that crime was, Eric had no idea. They had been friends in their youth and drifted apart. The exiled man was Italian, and Eric recalled that during their brief but intense friendship, Sergio, for that was his name, had been nervous around very young boys, and perhaps something had happened because of that. There was also another hint we discovered. In the flat's bedroom was a statue of a prepubescent boy holding a spray of flowers. The statue was carved of the purest white marble. It stood by the bed, and as we lay down his white almond shaped eyes stared emptily down upon us. His body was naked, his penis small. The presence of this object often made me sleep badly. As for the rest of the flat, the furniture was stark and simple, all of it in the darkest blue.

Ben was not happy without music, so he bought a record

player, and from various shops in Rome, built up a small collection. He was quiet with me most of the time and only after putting on a record of Nino Rota's music for *La Dolce Vita* did he literally dance with joy. This always happened after breakfast as we prepared for our day. With his skin clearer, I saw in his eyes as he was dancing, a shedding of his former reclusive self.

This was during the day, but in my nightly dreams another Ben was present. His body was not beautiful, and his naked flesh was covered in deep sores, some so deep that I saw the inside of his body. I saw his intestines tangled, strangling all passage of food, and his penis was a large hanging sore, burnt red by an inflammation. I clung to him and the smell of rotten meat, and I was transformed into a hungry insect, eating any part of his flesh that I desired. Then the dream would shift and his decaying body would cling to me, holding me down, his mouth without lips, just teeth; sharp teeth, sucking my cock and wrenching my balls from me, until there was only a painful gap there and blood pouring from it. I felt the agony of this and wanted to escape, but there was no escape. Only a loud scream of fear eventually woke me, and Ben would shake me and ask what was wrong. Then he would fall back into his own sleep, and I would stare up into the unseeing eyes of the statue looking pitilessly down on me. The scream of escape always came after dawn, and there was light in the room, but I was still immobilised by my nocturnal horrors. I could only stare at the statue and then up at the black beams that criss-crossed the ceiling of the room. As if by a miracle, breakfast erased the memory of all this. I was my normal self, and Ben was handsome, and his naked body (he liked to have his breakfast naked) paraded itself before me. He knew that the sexual passion between us was diminishing, and often with a mocking voice he would ask, "Wasn't it right to come here to this city that heals? I do not really believe in miracles, but how can I doubt that my face is better?"

And so we discovered more and more of this labyrinth of a

city with its winding River Tiber, like a rope of water ready either to drown love or bring life to it.

27

At the beginning of the third week, he asked me if he could go out sometimes alone. He had gone out alone before, but this time his voice was more emphatic about having his own solitary space and time. He gave no reason for this, and I felt suspicious. What does he need outside of us? I asked myself. Aren't I enough for him? But already I knew our sexual desire was in its death throes.

For a while I deluded myself and I tried to hold my thoughts on this at bay. But my pessimism reared its head again, and after a fourth excursion on his own he brought back the latest record of Françoise Hardy.

"I didn't know you liked her songs," I said.

"I do now."

"What do you mean *now*?"

"I heard this record in a shop."

"But I know enough about you to know that this is not your kind of music."

"My taste can change, can't it?" and he smiled at me. He looked happier than I had seen him for a long time.

I tried to shrug off the increasing doubts that were creeping into my mind.

"You are right, Ben. Tastes can change."

As we entered the fourth week, Ben was playing the same record every morning. Nino Rota had been put aside, and during that week he was out for the whole day three times. The other four days he reserved for me, but when we had lunch or dined, or went to museums, he had a lost look on his face. I sensed he was elsewhere. And in the fourth week he refused totally to have sex with me. When I asked why, he shrugged his shoulders and said, "It is what it is."

"What does that mean exactly?" I asked him.

"Too much repetition kills," he said.

"Couldn't we at least masturbate together?" I asked, feeling I was now grovelling.

"I can't get an erection with you anymore."

He sighed, and the sigh hit me like a heavy blow.

Paradoxically, with his denial of sex, my horror dreams ended. I slept well. Such is the mystery of passion, I told myself sarcastically.

28

The sun was fierce outside, and lying on the bed I had the drawings of Jesus, John and Judas scattered around me. The men in their passions, I said to myself, and beside the bed, the white statue looked down. I felt relaxed. My flesh naked. The room was my womb, and I was enfolded inside of it. I felt a gentleness of being, and that felt so much greater than love. As I looked at the drawings, I saw the men in their passions moving in an eternal stillness.

29

And so it was, the ending between Ben and myself. The fourth week stretched into the fifth week, and the money was just sufficient to afford that extra time. I spent little, but during the days when we were apart, he spent a lot, and I was given no explanation why. I saw that he had bought new, expensive clothes, and that his skin had improved to the point where the acne scars were almost non-existent. He would look in the mirror and proudly tell me that it was all gone and that his face was now perfect. This was not totally correct as the scars still showed, but by some willing blindness, he refused to see the reality. A vast improvement, yes, but not quite the perfection he perceived. So, why was it that I colluded with this and in a quiet madness, even my own mind saw him as being perfect?

This illusion of perfection was at its peak as he stood by Fontana dei Quattro Fiumi on the Piazza Navona. He was staring up at the Egyptian obelisk. His mouth was slightly open, and his flesh glowed.

"You are perfect," I said aloud.

"This is perfect," he said, pointing at the fountain. "All the passion of stone is there. Isn't this the best place in Rome?"

I had my camera with me and took a photo of him, standing as he was, upright like the obelisk, handsome and in awe of what he saw.

"We have passed it several times before, Ben."

"Yes, but I have never looked at it, never caught it to me. I feel I am at one with it."

The sun shifted in the sky, and small white clouds gathered. Time passed, and still he wanted to remain there.

"Can I be alone with it for a little longer?" he asked.

"I'll be back in half an hour," I replied.

"Yes," and his body moved nearer the fountain. The *yes* was said softly, as if I wasn't there, as if he was affirming something to the fountain and not to me.

I cannot remember where I walked, but I do remember that I felt heavy with loss. I knew that it was the beginning of the end of us, even as friends, and that our separate ways would never join again. I drank coffee at a café and looked at my watch. The half-hour was almost up, and I had no idea how many streets I had walked down. I paid, got up, and hurried back to him, and he was still there, in his own world, still captured by the beauty of the fountain. I tapped him on the shoulder, and as if coming out of a trance he smiled and suggested that we walk.

Eventually we entered the Chiesa di San Luigi dei Francesi, and looked at the three canvasses by Caravaggio. Then, like Judas, he kissed me on the mouth. No one else was in the church to see us.

"Caravaggio won't mind," he said, and he kissed me again, and then laughed.

30

I soiled my remaining feelings for him and did so quite deliberately. I was walking in the Villa Borghese Gardens and a youth smiled at me. He was leaning up against a tree and put his hands to his groin and rubbed himself in front of me. My flesh ached for sex, and I went up to him. He asked me, in Italian, if I wanted him.

"Yes," I replied in English.

"I speak English. Not well, but enough. So, what do you do here in our city?"

"I live."

I looked away from him.

"I live too," he replied. "I come here often. It is a good place to meet *stranieri*—strangers."

"How old are you?" I asked.

"Old enough. Sixteen."

"You look older."

"Maybe to you. Not to others. I like men, men like you. Older, but not old."

He took away his hands from his groin and I glanced down at the bulge in his jeans.

"Touch me if you want to," he said.

"Not here."

"Why not here? No one is around. This is a safe place."

"Do you know of any hotels where you can pay by the hour?" I asked.

"I live in a room in the suburbs. It is not the most beautiful part of Roma, but then, not everything can be beautiful, can it?"

"You are handsomely beautiful," I replied. He laughed at my remark, and I saw inside his mouth. I wanted to kiss his tongue.

It was very red, moistened by saliva.

He noticed my look and murmured, "You like my tongue? It is very thick and it licks well. Do you want to suck on it in a kiss?"

I nodded my head.

"Come closer," he said, and drew me to him.

"But the police?"

"They know me. Two of them have been with me. It is alright. Be free."

I sensed an innocent perversity in him, and bending forward I put my right hand to his mouth.

"Open it."

He smiled and opened his mouth wide.

"Put out your tongue as far as it can go."

"Like this?" There was laughter in his voice. His tongue was very wet, and I kissed it. I licked some of the saliva and it tasted good. My inner self whispered, he is from the earth. He is an earth boy. He wants you to take everything you want.

I pressed my body against him, and I repeated that I needed his tongue again. I drew it into my mouth and as gently as I could I bit on it, but accidentally I bit a little bit too hard and I drew blood. He did not react to this, and I continued sucking on his tongue for a long while, drinking from him, licking with my tongue against his, and he closed his eyes as I did so. At last, I drew back and whispered the word, "beautiful."

"Me?" and he laughed again.

"What's your name?"

"Bruno."

"Bruno, I want you to be my lover. I want to know every part of your body."

Was I taking my revenge on Ben by using the word *lover*? Or did I instinctively mean it?

"A lover is a lot," he replied.

"Can I be your lover for a while?"

"You want too much. I will be your lover if you allow me to have other men. I could not be happy with only one person."

"I understand," and I did. I also wanted to accept his terms. "I will pay you well."

He pushed me away from him, and I saw a different youth. With ferocity, he shouted at me, "I am not a whore. I am not like those boys who sell. Never, ever, will I accept money."

"But—"

"But what?" and with a rapid movement of his left hand, he struck me across the face. I jumped back and rubbed my face.

"It hurts, doesn't it?" he said. "I have big strong hands."

His voice was now low, and I heard a threat in what he was saying. This is the kind of boy who can kill, I thought.

We stayed in the same position for a few seconds until he broke the tension with a big laughing smile.

"You are not afraid of me," he cried out. "I like that. I will be your lover. So many are cowards, and you are not. If anyone goes too far with me, I hit them. And up until now they have all run."

We took a taxi to an outer suburb, run down, with piles of debris outside the buildings. Most of the windows were open and loud voices, babies crying, and men and women shouting echoed around us. He lived on the top floor of one of the better houses and he opened the door.

"Don't you have a key?"

"It was my brother's place. He got married. He has sex with me and permits me to live here for free."

I was shocked at this, and he hit me gently in the ribs.

"The look on your face! It would make the devil smile."

We entered the flat. It was basic, but clean. The windows had no shutters, and the light flooded in. Noticing again my look, he said, "Nothing to fear. No one can see in. Why have shutters?"

Taking me by the hand he took me to the only chair in the room. It was almost falling apart: old, deep and brown. I sank down into it.

"I hate furniture. Do you know something?"

"What?"

"I don't know your name."

"Jean-Paul."

"Français," he replied. "C'est bien."

His rough French accent delighted me.

"I am only half-French, Bruno."

"The sexy half, I hope. Now I make coffee for us in the kitchen. Relax."

"How many rooms are there here?" I asked.

"A bedroom, this room, and a kitchen and separate toilet. It is not big enough for a family, and my brother has already got two children, and it is cheaper than most of the flats in the building."

"How is it that you speak English so well?"

He smiled and came and sat on my lap.

"Shall we forget the coffee?" he asked. "But to answer your question, my brother teaches English. He is a clever man. He has always loved me with brotherly love and also with passionate desire. He taught me English when I was twelve, and after every lesson, he would fuck me. He has a big cock, like me, but he never wanted me to fuck him. I would like to fuck him. Maybe one day."

"How old was he when you were twelve?"

"Nineteen. Our parents are dead, and we are the only family. I have cousins, but they are distant in other cities, and so to increase the family, he got married. Not out of love, but he can pretend. Clara, his wife, is very much in love with him. He is a handsome man. He is my protector. But he also respects I like other men."

"Are *you* in love with him?"

"In love, in love, what does that mean. I love him, yes, because I have always known him. He goes with boys other than me. I am not jealous. He also goes with other women. I do not go with women."

"You are sixteen. You could change."

"I do not think of that. I do not want to suck on a woman's breast. I am not bisexual like my brother. I am completely male for a male. Now my friend, have we talked away sex for the moment?"

"Yes, for the moment, but let me kiss your tongue."
I grew to love his laughter, and he put out his tongue. I sucked on it and again drank him in.

"Some men drink my piss. Would you like that?"
I shook my head.

"It's okay. I find it boring to let them, but I do. I respect all kinds of desire."

He got up then, and whistling, he went to the kitchen.

"I have some *biscottini* with coffee. Would you like some?"
"Yes, Bruno."

"I think you like my name," he said, preparing the coffee.
"It's a strong name. I like it."

"It is short and hard, like my cock."

Then he did something that really surprised me. As the coffee was percolating, he took off his jeans. He was not wearing any underwear. Turning, he showed me his erect cock. It was thick, and it was long, and I wondered if I would be able to take it inside of me.

"You must see it first, what I have. If I am to be your lover, you should see. *D'accordo*?"

"D'accordo," and I smiled.

Bruno promptly put his jeans back on.

"You don't have to," I said. "You have a fine body."

"Do you want also to see my arse?"

"It can wait."

"No, no. I will show you. I want you to see all the essentials." With a slight sigh, he lowered his jeans again, and bending over, he showed me his firm young flesh. With his hands, he parted the cheeks and opened up to show me his hole. He widened it, and I saw the red interior, and like the red of his tongue, I wanted to go over and kiss it. "Do you like?" he asked.

"I want to kiss you there."

"Then do it."

I got up off the chair and going into the kitchen, fell to my knees, and pushing away his hands, I parted the cheeks myself. I licked around the orifice, then my tongue went in. I went as far as I could go, probing and kissing, then looked at the bright redness within. His beauty was overwhelming. I thought suddenly, he is teaching me the *earth* of loving. The *soil* of living, not in the excrement, but in the passage that makes way for it. I loved the taste, the smell. It smelt as if rain had fallen on it. A rain that increases the moisture of the land, and he was wet there, and I licked until I was exhausted.

"We have made love," I said, and fell back on the floor. He then covered my body with his own.

I have not shown my arse in this way before. Only you. You are the first, and I like it. Most men I have gone with show stupid disgust, and that is always when they think they go too far. Your tongue is also very long, and I liked it inside of me. You are my new lover, Jean-Paul. I think no one else will be like you."

We kissed for a long time, and then we had coffee with small round biscuits, buttery in taste, and played a special game, mashing them in our mouths, kissing and sharing each other's food.

"You really are the earth," I said.

"You are also a poet, I like that. Have you just discovered the earth?"

"Yes, after many years."

"Can you be satisfied with what the earth offers?"

"With you, yes."

"No, not just with me. If I have other lovers, then so must you. The earth is for everyone that loves it." He paused and said, "The day is passing. Come to me the day after tomorrow. This is just the beginning. We are in no hurry. Be like a Roman, Jean-Paul. Hurrying is a crime."

31

I contacted Eric. I had made my decision to stay in Rome. I told him that Ben and I had reached the point where we would have to part.

"I am sorry," he said.

"We rarely see each other, and as for our lovemaking, it is non-existent."

"I think you should ponder over this. I know Ben very well. Sometimes I believe he loves in the mind and not in the flesh. If you can accept that I think he will stay with you."

I was not sure what to say.

"Eric, I want to make my home here. I need work. I am learning Italian, but it is slow."

"I love you, Jean-Paul. You should have your wish, whatever happens between you and Ben. I will send you a couple of thousand. Let's say I bet on the horses yesterday and won," he laughed. "But seriously, accept the money. I can also help you get established. I know of two families who want an English teacher. One of them is serious about learning, the other wants only to hear an English voice reading poetry."

I laughed with him.

"Eric, thank you," I said.

"Consider it only a small thing that I am doing. But on condition that I can visit you in Rome. I love it and I hate it. It is superficiality with depth. Now figure that one out! All that Baroque and posing. And yet—" and he paused.

"And yet what, Eric?"

"It has life. The money will arrive within the week, and I will praise you to the skies in a few phone calls to those families."

"Will I be safe with them?" I joked.

"I think one of the families has a gay son. If there is no attraction, tease him. His name is Carlo. He is not bad-looking, and neither is he good-looking. He will be thirty by now and he may have found a permanent partner, which is a difficult thing to do in Rome. He is the one who likes poetry. He will make you read Shelley, and then he will bore you to tears with Leopardi. So many other poets in Italy, but unless he has changed, he ignores them."

I laughed so much at this I cried.

"That's better," Eric said.

"You are the best of them all," I replied, and the conversation ended. By the end of the week I had the money, plus appointments with both families. I almost considered myself a Roman citizen.

32

When Ben realised I had more money and two jobs of work he became enthusiastic about me once more. He even took me to one of Rome's more expensive restaurants where the food was appallingly bad, but still people had to be seen there. It was in the restaurant that I noticed a small ring on his small right finger.

"I've never seen that before," I said.

"I liked the look of it. Normally I am not attracted to rings, but this was inexpensive in a second-hand shop. I thought it would bring me luck. So I bought it, and put it on a finger that it felt good on."

He smiled at me. I didn't believe him.

"Is that the truth?"

"Why should I lie to you?"

"Everyone lies," I replied, and as I said that I saw Ben shrug his shoulders.

"Everyone! Everyone! You always generalise, Jean-Paul. That's a profound generalisation that means nothing at all."

I picked at my food. It had already grown cold.

"Everyone *does* lie," I repeated. I suddenly felt angry. The meal had become a disaster. I knew the ring had another meaning for him. He loathed rings. "If I had bought it for you, would you have accepted it?"

He smiled again. The same old, cold smile.

"What do you want me to say?"

"The truth. Would you have accepted that gold ring from me?"

"This is getting boring," he replied. "Can we make it on to coffee? The food is inedible now that it's not hot."

"Are you in a hurry to end this evening?"

"No, it's just that I don't like cold food when it's meant to be hot." He paused, then added, "You really want us to row, don't you?" and the smile was gone.

"Not particularly, but at least it could be a passionate row. That I would like. Passion has died between us. A row could perhaps revive the death of sex. We are in Rome. The number one place for believing in miracles."

Ben pushed his plate aside, and without answering, called one of the waiters over. He ordered coffee.

Then I suddenly said it.

"You have a lover."

He glanced at me. A furtive glance. Then he sighed.

"So you really *do* want a row."

"No, Ben, I want the truth from you. First the facts. Now that I have money, you offer me your time. And you do love money! But I don't think you care for me or even like me anymore."

"Idiot," he said, and put the hand with the ring on it over my hands. "We'll have sex tonight," he said. "We can look at your French porno drawings and then have sex. We could even play a game. Who should I be? Jesus or John?"

The coffee arrived, and instead of drinking it I reached for the bottle of wine we had drunk only a little from, put the bottle to my mouth and drank, and drank. I felt my mind grow bolder, clearer. I put the bottle down.

"That's a vulgar way of drinking," he said.

"You can be Judas," I replied.

"He's the voyeur, isn't he? How can I pretend to be him?"

"Easily," I replied. "I will be Jesus, and just have a wank, while you watch."

Ben leant back in the plush red chair he was seated on, a colour as rich as a cardinal's robes. He stared at me, a vacant stare.

"If you want," he said casually.

"Do you know why I am thinking of Judas?"

"You will no doubt tell me."

"Because you are a betrayer at heart. Only your acne stopped you from being so before."

"So?"

"You are going with another man. Or maybe more. Don't lie."

There was a short silence.

"Alright," he shouted at me, and some of the people at other tables looked at us. A waiter hurried over as if the word *alright* was a command for him. In expensive restaurants, everything gets confused and eventually turns to farce. I shook my head at him, and he retreated.

"You want the truth, and you can have it. His name is Sandro. He is better looking than you, and he is a dermatologist. Who do you think I went to see during those days we weren't together? He is attracted to me, and in my own way, I am attracted to him."

"And you get free treatment."

"Of course. He loves me."

"And what about you? Is his love returned?"

"I told you he's good-looking. He's in his forties, but looks younger. Personally, I would have preferred someone in their twenties, but I knew he could do so much for my face."

"You really are a little shit, aren't you?"

"Oh dear, do we have to resort to nastiness?"

He gave another very long sigh. I was so fucking tired of his sighs. It was so theatrical. A scene in a play where the young lead has to act even though he can't. I imagined the sigh echoing all around the restaurant, and the rest of the people in it, staring up at the stage, which was of course our table.

"But you are, aren't you," I continued. "A golden piece of shit. And this guy Sandro put that ring on your finger. Nothing to commit himself with, but done in the Roman way of a rich gesture. He is rich, of course. I don't want any denial that he isn't."

"He has money, yes. But there is a meanness about him that

I don't quite like. I've tried every trick in the book, but somehow I don't get the amount I need."

"But your face and body have improved because of him. You could get money. You could get money out of anyone."

"I would like a Cognac."

I gestured towards the waiter, who with a look of impatience on his face, returned to our table, took the order, and within what seemed seconds, returned with the Cognac.

Ben drank it down quickly. He then turned round and looked at the waiter who was at a distance.

"He's poor. Don't tantalise him by looking at him. You're better looking than he is, and if he is gay, he will in his own way respond, and I don't want to be made a fool of at this table."

"I don't mind the poor," Ben said.

"You really have become a little snob since you came to Rome, haven't you?"

Ben yawned, then smiled. He said nothing in return.

"How do you think Eric would react now if he was here? He loves you more than anyone else, and you know it."

Getting up, Ben walked away from the table towards the toilets. I waited for his return, but he took his time. After half an hour, I realised what had happened. Ben was quite flagrant about having sex with the waiter when he eventually returned. His hair was messed up and his face was flushed.

"Bisexual!" he said as he sat in front of me. "Such a shy boy."

"You slut!" I stood up.

"What?" he asked.

"Pay the bill!"

I hurried out of the restaurant and walked for several hours. I walked by the River Tiber and when I reached Castel Sant'Angelo I felt exhausted and retraced my steps. Rome looked cleansed by the first sight of dawn.

33

I spent most of my free time with Bruno, but more on that later. I had work to do. Each family welcomed me on their own terms. They both lived near the Piazza del Popolo, but were unaware of each other's proximity. They were not as Eric had described. The supposedly gay son of one of the families was straight, and very demanding, sucking up the English language like a vampire. I will not describe either family in detail. They paid me and I did my job well. But let me pause on one idiosyncrasy. In every room of their vast homes, and yes, they had sufficient wealth for such a privilege, were portraits and photographs of the Pope. Large and small, he was there, everywhere, and I had to avert my eyes as I taught. I asked the kindest among them, a young woman named Belinda, why there were so many.

"We are fervent believers," she said in her near-perfect English, "and we love our Pope very much."

"But surely one is enough?"

There was no answer to that. We changed the subject.

34

I was sitting in a café, but I cannot recall where. The sun was too hot, and I was overwhelmed by the heat. I looked at the people passing by. I did not want to sit on the terrace, and chose instead a table just inside where I could look out of a window. I was mesmerised by the sight of so many bodies, all seen from the outside by others; and how impenetrable it was that their flesh covered their inner selves. What does anyone know of the inner selves of others, I thought, what they dream of at night, and even during the day. We speak to people, even those closest to us, but it is only a veneer of the self; the sheen of the self with words that probably do not have any resemblance to the words inside that dictate their panics, their fears, their happiness, their illusions. And as I stared, I saw a woman pick up a piece of paper from the ground, and watched as she put it into her jacket pocket. I wanted to rush to her and ask her why. The paper had nothing to do with her, yet she wanted it. I had seen the paper before, trodden over by others, dirty in appearance, and yet this well-dressed woman wanted it, had to have it. Had she lost it a while back and returned to search for it? Who could know, and there was only conjecture. Her face was as crumpled as the paper, as if she was about to crack up, to collapse. She moved on and disappeared into the crowd. No one looked at her or thought it bizarre, but carried on with their outer chatter and probable banalities. No, we do not *know* others. We can never penetrate that carapace of the flesh to the interior within; intrude, search out their deepest beings. I thought of those dying. We, those who will grieve, often have no conception of the dying person's thoughts, their peace or their turmoil. We see only an outer agony, or an outer peace, but what of within? We know nothing. We know nothing of the being of animals or how they sense life; not really, despite all our experiments to find the meaning of a bird's song or why an insect stays petrified when we approach. It, the animal, knows; it *must* think, but what? We will never know, except that by all appearances, they must. Fear, dread, a silence of the moving self. I, the outer me, thought these thoughts as I sat inside the café without a name, and I was petrified that I would die, never knowing who or what was really going on inside of me. I empathised with all those others, all of this world we call the earth, for knowing only the superficiality of being. Rome, it seemed to me was the epitome of this loneliness, this separation from the essential and happier perhaps *not* to know. Laughter sprayed the air like a jet from a fountain, and within that source of laughter was nothing that could be known. I felt I was going mad with the pain and the joys of existing. I caught the attention of the waiter, but I could not speak. I wanted to pay, but my body could not move. He was patient and watched me. I stared up at him and he stared down at me. Who am I? I wanted to ask him. He moved away, his patience gone. And then, like a light, beating open inside of me, I could move again, and join again the civilisation that surrounded me. I paid my bill and then I knew I had to see a Raphael painting. I needed Raphael. The artist so much better, or so I thought, than all the others, who could capture an instant of time, and even instances out of time. I wanted his stillness and his perception, and the beauty within and without of his work.

I went to the Pantheon. Here was his burial space, then on to the Vatican's Pinacoteca. I stared up at *La Trasfigurazione*: Christ's momentary ascent from the mountain. I paid no notice to Elijah and Moses. He was above both, and to me his face was totally single. He was not *my* Jesus, the Jesus of my drawings, but a radiance beyond all comprehension. Could I *know* and who *could* know the moment of His being, so still in motionless ascent, but to what sphere? I looked at the figures below; their thoughts, their images of this outside of time experience. And I could not know. Raphael caught the moment for ever. I only knew that all of us know nothing of this, except to be caught in the splendour of colour and the beauty of Raphael's art.

35

I rang Eric. He said he was not well. Then he asked me how I was getting on. I told him about the two families and how much they resembled each other without knowing it.

"Oh, it's my fault," he said quietly. "I got mixed up. The families I told you about, I knew long ago. The two families I sent you to were seeking help more recently from a man I met in Rome who now lives most of his time in London. You see, my mind is going. Memory plays tricks with me." He paused, then added, "And to top it all, I can recall him saying that they were decidedly far-right. He describes anyone in love with the Vatican as far-right, and these ones sound religious to the point of mania. Are they giving you any trouble?"

"No, but it seems strange that both houses have pictures of the Pope in each room."

He laughed, which brought on a fit of coughing.

"How awful!" he managed to say. "All that money and they can't make space for a Tintoretto or a Botticelli."

"I don't think even they could afford that!" I said laughingly.

"Have any of them tried to seduce you? Fanatics often do. It's all because of the sexual frustration they feel while holding the hand of Christ! Oh dear, maybe someone is listening in to our conversation on the phone. The English are still hot on blasphemy."

"One of them *is* nice," I replied.

"Male or female?" Eric asked.

"Female."

"No pretty boys?"

"None."

"Shame on me for sending you there!"

"Her name is Belinda, and her English is almost as good as ours. I think one day she will break away and hopefully marry someone from the wrong side of the Coliseum."

I wanted to tell Eric about Bruno, but knowing he was not well, I did not want him to worry about what he might consider to be a complication.

"Jean-Paul, maybe this Belinda has set her sights on you. You're handsome enough, and many Italians would adore to move to England. I know quite a few who dream of places like Arundel. *And* she would have enough money to pay for everything. You could be a kept husband."

"Stop teasing, Eric."

"Oh, indulge me. I am sick as Hades, and I only have my doctor to hold my hand."

"I could tell Ben you are unwell. He has, by the way, fallen for a dermatologist."

I thought he would never stop laughing when he heard this.

"It won't last," he said. "It won't last. Now I've got a pain in my heart." Then in a more sombre voice, he added, "Ben was a pain in my heart. Oh, how he carried those spots on his back like a cross! Or has the dermatologist relieved him of them?"

I wanted to stop talking about Ben, but Eric prevented me from doing so.

"Do you know the man's name? I could look him up. I have my spies in Rome. If that man is playing with him I will—well, what will I do? Kill him?"

"Don't bother. He has his treatment and the man's money when he can get it."

"Yes, it's foolish of me not to think of that. But I believe he desires you and will be faithful in his fashion."

"I don't want his fucking fashion. I want something better. Purer."

Eric laughed at this.

"But Jean-Paul, he *is* pure in his own way. He has suffered. It takes a long while to learn from suffering. But I know he has exaggerated a little about his affliction."

I took another route in the conversation and urged Eric to come to Rome as soon as he was feeling better. I told him that he had to; that it was an order. Our conversation continued, and we said many things to each other, and I didn't care at all how much the call was costing. I wanted Eric near me, even more so in a way than Bruno's nearness. Bruno, hopefully, was my future. Eric was the *now* of my life. The sun set as I put the phone back on its receiver.

I slept badly that night and around eleven the following morning I got a call. A man called Jonathan told me that Eric had died in his sleep. He went on to explain that Eric had given him my number a while back, and had apparently said, "Just in case. Just in case of an emergency."

"Will you let me know about the funeral?"

"He wants no one there," Jonathan replied. "He told me he wanted to be completely alone in that final disappearance."

I burst into tears, and Jonathan became flustered. I apologised and with a brief thank you and a goodbye, I put down the phone.

It rang an hour later, but I did not answer.

36

I want so much to relate more of the beginnings and the outcome of my relationship with Bruno, but the doors must be closed on Ben before I do so.

A week after Eric's death, Ben rang me.

"Things are going badly for me," he said. "Can we meet up?"

I realised, of course, that he must have heard of Eric's death, and that he was grieving. When I met him at an open-air café near the Spanish Steps, I saw that he was angry.

"Couldn't you be bothered to contact me?" he asked.

"I'm sorry, but grief has kept me away from all contact, either on the phone or in person, with anyone, and I assumed that like me you would have been notified of his death."

This was completely true. I hadn't seen anyone. I hadn't even contacted Bruno.

"Someone called Jonathan contacted me. I have no idea how he got my telephone number. A total stranger."

"He rang me too."

"And no bloody funeral! I could have done with a break. Rome is getting me down. Why did Eric behave like this? How did he even find out my current number? I suppose you must have told him I was living with a dermatologist, and knowing Eric, he acted immediately and found out who that dermatologist was. Did you tell him?"

"Yes, I told him you were living with a dermatologist."

"Oh, that's a nice conspiracy! Now I feel more alone than ever. Even you are alienated from me."

I sensed no grief at all over Eric, and I told him so.

"You expect me to sob into my coffee? I suppose you

believe I should react in that way? Well, I don't. He's dead. Grief brings no one back."

"That's one way of looking at it."

"He left me nothing in his will, did you know that? He was supposedly in love with me. Passionately in love with me. And now that he's gone, I realise I meant nothing to him."

Impatiently I stood up and stared at the ascending steps. I could no longer bear hearing Ben or looking at him. I stared up at the Chiesa della Trinità dei Monti. I wanted to walk away, but then I felt a pull on my arm, and Ben cried out, "I don't matter anymore to anyone."

"What about your dermatologist? Sorry, I don't know his name."

"Well, it seems Eric knew his name, and as for the man you call my dermatologist, he *does* want me, but at the same time, I don't matter. He never gives me enough money."

I had turned away from the Steps and looked at Ben's face. A bitter thought struck me: he looked older than the buildings of Rome. They too had marks on them, but they had a rough beauty I responded to. Ben's face was still slightly marked despite all the improvements, but his eyes were cold. I felt sorry for him and felt no attraction.

"Did Eric leave you any money?" he asked.

"I don't think that is any of your business."

"So, you're brushing me off, just like that."

His voice was suddenly resigned, and he seemed to fall in upon himself.

"What do you want from me, Ben? Are you attempting to return to me?"

"Would you have me back? I would try to be faithful."

"Let's walk," I replied.

"Alright."

We walked through the city, stepping into a few churches, and finally I bought him a meal. We said next to nothing to each other. He drank a lot of wine and then quite suddenly put his hand on my knee, and then moved it up to my thigh.

"I'm a bit of a shit, aren't I?" he said. "You told me I was a piece of golden shit."

"I exaggerated, Ben."

"Then fall in love with me again."

I paid the bill and suggested a visit to the Galleria Doria Pamphilj.

"More Caravaggios?" he replied with a sad smile.

"Yes."

"Then I'll say no to the offer. Couldn't we go back to your place? We could be alone together."

"No, we can't, Ben. You've hit the nail on the head. I don't want to be *alone* with anyone at the moment. Maybe we would have sex, but we would each be alone in it."

"Then I can't offer anything more to you, can I?"

"I will remain your friend," I replied, knowing full well that we couldn't be.

"And would you, could you, help me financially when I need it? The fear of not having money is terrible. Eric was good to me. But he's gone."

"You are young, good-looking, and you are intelligent. Meet other people. Finish with Rome if you have to. Get a job back in England."

"Eric betrayed me. How can I return to London? London would always remind me of that. He *could* have left me something!"

"He loved you too much. That is all I know, Ben."

We walked some more and finally ended up at the Vatican. In the shadow of one of the colonnades, he kissed me, then held me at arm's length.

"That's to say goodbye, Jean-Paul," he said. "I'll survive."

And he walked away from me.

37

Bruno was not offended by my infrequent visits. He always welcomed me as if it were the first time. I recalled his words, "Be like a Roman, Jean-Paul. Hurrying is a crime." It was not until Eric's money arrived in the bank that my visits were more concentrated. It's strange, as I have gone so far in these recollections and not mentioned that he was blond. He had the rather haughty, and proud look that many northern Italian blonds have. But then again perhaps that is yet another generalisation.

"Does your brother look like you?" I asked him when we were lazily lying on the floor together, our bodies half-dressed, and sweat covering our flesh.

"Eventually you will see for yourself. Now we eat. Cheese, bread and wine. What more do we need?"

"I want to consume your body again. It is all the food I need, Bruno."

"No. We eat. I need more than sperm in my mouth to satisfy me."

He leapt up as I tried to grasp him, and arranging his rather torn and well-worn clothes, he went into the kitchen. He left the door open so that I could hear him.

"We have no cheese. Can you go to the shop?"

"I don't know where the shops are around here."

"*Cretino*! Come over to me. Your hair is too neat. I don't want the shopkeepers to see a man who is too elegant."

"That's snobbery," I replied.

"Come here!"

The last words were said as a command. I liked to be commanded by Bruno who looked so much older than his years. His skin was the skin of a man, rough, gentle and sometimes soft. He never reached out for me with gestures of tenderness. He would just grab me like the cute animal he was. I went into the kitchen.

Mockingly I scolded him for calling me an idiot, and with a swipe of his right hand he hit me across the face.

"I have pictures of my family in Mussolini's army. Soldiers. They would laugh and salute before they executed people. My grandfather on my father's side was murdered like that by his cousin. Killed because he was a communist. He did not believe in Soviet Russia, but he believed in a true communism, and they shot him in the head. I think of him now dying, and seeing that salute before they did what they did. And these soldier gods were supported by the Vatican! I have an element of the soldier in me. I give orders. I hit you, but I hit you gently. I do not apologise."

I rubbed my face. His hit had perhaps been harder than he intended.

"I'm sorry about your family's past," I said.

"Now you know. And now you go and fetch cheese. Ripe cheese. In France they have cheese so ripe it has maggots crawling all over. One day when I have a passport, I want to go to France and eat that cheese."

"Did you really have to hit me?" I asked.

"I do not apologise. It's anger. I have much anger inside of me. Perhaps I hate myself because most of my family were fascists. I know I have the same blood as them." Then he stared at me in the eyes. "I am as I am. Leave me if you want to."

"I can't do that, Bruno."

"Thank you for saying that. Now, go and buy us some cheese. My belly is angry as well."

I found a shop that specialised in cheese. It was dirty. There was dog shit on the floor, and the place smelt. The man behind the counter was bearded and dirty as well. In bad Italian, I asked for the kind of cheese Bruno liked. He looked at me suspiciously.

"English?" he asked.

"Yes."

"Your Italian bad."

"I know that. Now can I pay?"

He pulled the money out of my hand and spat on the floor at the same time.

I said in English, "There is shit on the floor." I pointed to the mess.

"I do clean. I am not dirty. It is from an old woman, alone with a dog. The dog is—oh, what is the word for it?"

"Incontinent?" I replied.

"I have learnt a new word. Incontinent," and he wrapped the cheese in brown paper. He then gave me a friendly smile.

"I hope to stay in Rome," I said.

He laughed very loudly.

"You *hope*? Why you hope? Stay or go, but not hope. Ridiculous word, hope."

I laughed, and then we both laughed together. After a while, after many visits to the shop, we were almost friends. If the shop was empty, he would ask for a short English lesson.

"I would like to go to America one day," he told me one afternoon when the shop was full of flies settling happily on the cheese. "But I think it is too clean. I am clean, but I do not want to be more than clean. I like to be clean in my own way. I think Americans wash too much. Maybe I won't go."

His name was Guido, and he was full of contradictions.

"I don't need America," he said to me weeks after. "I am afraid I will look stupid. All beautiful shops in America. Not like mine. I want to open one like mine, or have a stall in a market. I like the flies and the dust. Dust is clean."

Every time I saw him there was laughter in our voices. I told Bruno about him.

"He is an old man. He is nearly seventy. America will not want him. Better he stays here. He is known here. There he will be just a number. America, a fascist country anyway. They pretend democracy."

"He's nice to me," I replied.

"I don't *not* like him, but he is stupid."

"There is nothing stupid in wanting to improve yourself. He is clearly still full of adventure. He wants to learn English. When I have time, I give him lessons."

Bruno came and kissed me on the mouth.

"I am glad you are not an old man," he said.

"Won't you care for me when I am old?"

"We will both be dead. Atomic bomb. Rome will be another Hiroshima."

I laughed at this, but unlike Guido, Bruno did not like to be laughed at.

"Why I care for you I do not know," he said angrily. Then he slowly pushed his body against mine and fiercely forced me down onto the floor. He fucked me. He farted when he came. I was used to his farts. I smelt the earth and wanted to take him to the countryside and for us to bathe each other in wet mud.

That night I dreamt of England. I was half-asleep and I heard birdsong. I drifted between waking and sleeping, borne along on the song. I was in England, and the suburbs of Rome were far from me. I tried to identify the bird's sound. No, I thought, the trill was different; no, it's so complex that no composer could ever attain its perfection, or even the greatest of singers achieve such a sound. All the rest was silence. Only the song and being close to Bruno as I surfaced in a haze from the dream, then plunging back into it again. In the silence with only the bird's song I saw trees; a scattered number of trees bordering the curves of a winding road and then I saw a bush and it was there that the bird was hidden from me. How fine were those narrow lanes so prevalent in Sussex. Lonely places, not of loneliness, but of fullness and still the bird sang for me. Then on a fading note it stopped. I saw the winding road, lanes leading off it, and silence in its totality. I saw the last gold rays of the late evening sun, hawthorn too, glowing in a white splash, and somehow I knew the bird was asleep, that bird I could not identify.

38

A few days later I asked Bruno if he would like to travel to some other places in Italy with me. He pouted, which he often did when he was doubtful.

"I would only like to see Firenze," he said.

I looked out of the window. I did not like Florence very much. I would have preferred to go further south. The sky from the window was a molten blue. Its liquid air running over the houses, making the desolation (or beauty) of the suburbs blue. Further south it would flow even more, and I imagined it washing over everything. What painter was it who used blue so much the images were nearly totally saturated? I saw a woman, Mary, mother of Jesus, all variations of blue, the face obscured, turning away from the viewer. This painter loved each shade and variation of blue; clothes in folds of sky blue, other clothes the colour of the deepest blue of the sea. I had seen his work, or had it been in a dream? I dreamt so much in Italy. With a sigh I thought, I will take Bruno to Florence if he wants that, but what did he especially want to see there? I had visited the city years before with one of my French lovers, before the flood of 1966 which had destroyed so much. I recalled seeing Cimabue's *Crucifix* before the onslaught of mud and water. The *real* Jesus was in that work; the twisted body, blood flowing in that final agony on the cross. So thin, the loincloth, I could see his genitals. I saw a man, only a man, tortured by nails, his stomach bloated with fear and displaced guts.

"You look at the sky. Look at me! Can we go to Firenze?"

"I imagine much of the city is still a shadow of its former self," I replied. "But maybe they have restored sufficiently for it to be almost as fine as it was before."

"I have a friend there. Giorgio. He is my brother's friend as well. He nearly drowned in the flood. Now he shuts himself away. My brother would like me to see him, talk to him, persuade him to come to Rome."

"Supposing he doesn't want to see anyone yet? Traumas can last a long time."

"Oh, big word trauma. He is himself. So far, neither me nor my brother have been able to go to Firenze."

"Do you want me to stay in a hotel while you stay with him? If the answer is yes, then I can give you the money to go alone."

"I am not a *marchetta*! I am with you, Jean-Paul. We stay a few days. In the afternoon, *you* will see all the places tourists like."

"I have been there, Bruno. I am not going as a tourist."

The word tourist upset me. I was not an official resident, it was true, but I was not a tourist. I told Bruno how I felt. Bruno pouted again and looked at the floor.

"I say everything wrong," he said.

"No, it's me being over-sensitive. The sky is falling down on us with its beauty everywhere in Italy. Can you be ready tomorrow?"

Bruno laughed. He opened his mouth wide, and I wanted again to lick and kiss his red tongue.

"You are so funny with your images. Are all Englishmen poets. The sky is not falling. We have skies full of clouds. Perhaps we have clouds when we arrive in Firenze."

His English was getting better each day. His knowing mind learnt quickly.

"I will be your poet," I said.

"No, it is for old men and women. I want your cock, your arse. I do not want poetry about it. I want the flesh of you. I want all of you in the flesh. There is no other way for me."

"You *have* read poetry," I said.

He shrugged his shoulders.

"*M'illumino d'immenso*," he said. "That's all I know. Everyone knows those words. They are by Ungaretti. *Mattina*. They are beautiful words."

"Like today." I pointed at the sky. "What else is that sky but those two untranslatable lines?"

"*Stupido*," and he put out his tongue.

We fucked in the heat by the window, and at my climax, I looked at the blue above. Then I turned to look at Bruno.

"You are full of contradictions," I whispered in his ear.

"Of course."

"And I sense you know other poems. Stop pretending."

"Oh, shut up."

39

Florence looked distinctly drab. Before leaving Rome, I bought a copy of E.M. Forster's *A Room with a View*. I loved the book, but the *pensione* I stayed in was not at all like the Pensione Bertolini in his novel. It was a run-down place, hidden away in some fortress house, so typical of Florence, and all I had to look at was a wall. The bed was hard. Breakfast was provided. But the option of an evening meal, I avoided. I had seen visitors eating when I arrived early in the evening. They looked unhappy, and no one was talking. On their plates I saw pieces of meat in a greenish sauce, and I watched as an old woman raised her fork to her mouth and bit on the meat with a look of revulsion. I took her unspoken advice and told the indifferent man who looked at my passport that I would eat elsewhere. He stared at me without replying, then scribbled something on a notepad beside him. Paranoia set in and I thought when I entered my room facing a black wall that this man was punishing me for either being English or for refusing their food.

Bruno had gone to stay with his brother's friend, and during the days that we stayed there we met only for an hour each day in a café near the Ponte Vecchio. I have not mentioned the rain which poured down relentlessly for three days, and still paranoid I wondered if this was a portent of a new disastrous flood. Bruno had no raincoat, and when I asked if I could buy one for him, he shrugged and said he liked the rain.

"But you are used to the heat of Rome," I said.

"So?"

"Well, you like the heat, don't you? You always say how much you love it."

"Are we going to have an argument?" he asked.

"Of course not. I'm worried about you catching cold, falling ill."

"You English! We have one hour, and we talk about the weather. Can't you see I am fit and strong? I am not the kind who ever falls ill. I am immune to illness."

"None of us are immune."

"So you *do* want an argument."

"Bruno, I *hate* this constant rain. I am running into so many buildings to get away from it." I was not wearing a raincoat, but I did have an umbrella. As the rain fell vertically and there was no wind, I was protected.

"Where do you go during the days?" he asked.

"I spend most of my time in the Uffizi Gallery."

"I have never been there. I think there are Botticellis, no?"

Changing the subject, I asked him how his brother's friend was.

"Giorgio is living like a pig."

"Pigs are clean," I said.

"Now make fun of me. I am not ignorant of farm life."

I tried another approach to my question, asking if Giorgio had enough food; whether he was looked after by anyone who visited and helped him.

"Of course," he replied sharply.

"Then why are you there?" I asked.

"I am following my brother's wishes. How many times do I have to explain? I gave Giorgio the money you gave me, and all he said was, 'How can I spend it? I never want anything.' I told you it was a bad situation. Do I have to repeat he was nearly drowned. He is afraid of everything. The room he lives in is an attic. He says if the flood comes again, it will not reach him. He only feels safe there."

"Another flood is unlikely," I replied.

"Who are you? God?"

"I said unlikely. I did not say it was beyond possibility. Looking at this constant rain, I too have my doubts."

Bruno looked tired and I told him so.

"I sleep on the floor. One blanket. No pillow. Yes, I am tired."

Then I saw tears in his eyes, and he saw that I noticed them. He rubbed his eyes vigorously.

"I care deeply for you," I said gently. "I think you are good in doing what you do for him."

"We talk. That's all. He is—oh fuck, I forgot the word—near collapse. I am afraid he will collapse if he continues for much longer."

"Now I am going to make you angry," I said.

"What are you going to say?"

"He needs medical help."

Bruno looked down at the table. He looked at the cold cup of coffee. I had also bought him a sandwich, but he did not eat, and he did not drink. He said he would keep the sandwich for later.

"And you are not eating properly. You like lots of food. Remember?"

"I told you I am strong. One time in my life, I did not eat for a week. No money. I couldn't. I survived. I slept. I am not hungry when I am sleeping."

"And does Giorgio sleep?"

"He has bad dreams. He keeps me awake."

"Bruno, I repeat, he needs to go to a hospital. He needs medical help."

There was a long silence between us. His face looked worn out. I saw the old man that he would eventually become. The future was in the present, and I was afraid. I cursed his brother for stupidly sending him to see his friend. The tide of future time was washing all over Bruno. I had seen children in my life who looked old, faces creased up, wrinkled, sad. I realised too that Bruno was only a sixteen. I felt a sudden brutal sense of shame in wanting his body, in desiring him.

"What shall I do?" he asked, breaking the silence. He sounded defeated.

"I will tell you what I would do in this situation." Then I paused. I did not want his anger again.

"Continue."

"Bruno, ring a hospital. You know this city better than I do. Find out the best help for him. I will pay for any expenses."

I felt suspicious about the government not helping. How did Giorgio get his money, if he was not officially sick. If there was no record that he was sick. And as for savings, if he had any, they must have depleted over the years. I brushed the suspicions aside, but I was troubled by having them. I then asked Bruno how he got his money.

"Giorgio has a lot of savings, but I will think about what you say." He spoke quietly, his voice worn with defeat.

"You have done your best, Bruno. He needs help. Objective help."

"My brother expects more from me. He would not like Giorgio to be in an institution."

"He needs objective help from people who are trained to help. You have come here, but you are not trained for this."

"I know," he murmured.

"And remember, he has been in this state since 1966. Years of fear."

"I know, I know."

"We are in the third day here. Leave me now and try to get in touch with a hospital or rest home. He will have the right care. Trust me."

"I want sex with you," he said. Then surprisingly, he grinned at me."

"Back in Rome, Bruno."

"I know of a cheap hotel. Quick sex."

"No, go back to Giorgio and make those calls. I am not only here because I want to have sex with you, but because I am a friend as well. I am your passionate friend, and care for you in every way."

He nodded his head.

"Have you some money on you?" he asked.

I gave him all that I had. Fortunately, I had taken some out of the bank.

"That is too much," he said. "I am not with you for your money."

"You may need a taxi to a hospital. You may need many things. Be stronger than strong, Bruno. You can do it. Make your brother understand it all later." Then, like an inner snake, the suspicions slid back.

He smiled at me. A smile that looked relaxed.

"I will do it," he said, and his face was young again.

His hands were dirty, and his blond hair needed a wash. Perhaps rashly, as others were nearby, he quickly kissed me on the mouth. His tongue flicked against mine. I tasted peppermint.

"Peppermint drops! It keeps me alive," and he laughed.

Then he was gone, disappearing into the rainy day.

40

Did I betray Bruno? So long ago, and I still do not know. I was sexually frustrated, and late the same day I went with an older, handsome man, a blond German who was looking at the Duomo, a guidebook in his hands. He had the book open, and was glancing at it and then at the cathedral. I went and stood beside him. He smiled at me.

"Incredible, isn't it?"

He said this in German, and I apologised and replied that I came from England. He had a very soft voice when he repeated his words in English.

Edging nearer to him I brushed against his raincoat. The rain had eased up a little, and I saw that his heavily used guidebook was in a poor state. He saw me glance at it, and I felt him press against me.

"This book is very old," he said. "It's ruined. I don't know why I use it. I know this place well enough. But there are always some details in it that help me to know more."

"So, this is not your first visit?" I asked.

"No, I have been here several times. I love this city. I am planning on moving here. And you?"

"I am planning on living in Rome."

"I'm not one for *la dolce vita*," he replied. There was laughter in his voice as he said this. "I'm also not crazy about all that baroque."

"I like the atmosphere there."

"Are you married?"

"No."

"Me neither. I'm sorry if my accent is hopelessly American. I had a lover who was American, and I guess I caught the bug of speaking English badly with him."

"I'm Paul," I said, for some reason deliberately not wanting to explain that I had a French side to me.

"Heinrich," he replied and stuffed the guidebook into his raincoat pocket. Then he asked quickly, "Are you free for the rest of the day?"

"Yes," I said. Inside of me, I apologised to Bruno. I reminded myself that both Bruno and I were free to go with others. I also told myself this is only a small crime of passionate need.

"Are you staying near here?" he asked, and there was a slight gasp in his throat. I could already feel the heat of his need.

"I'm staying in a very bad pensione. I could have chosen an hotel, but then I thought of E.M. Forster's *Room with a View*, and imagined a suitably romantic place."

"I don't know the book. But clearly it has not met your expectations."

I laughed.

"No, the pensione is filthy and the place smells of very badly cooked food. It's just no good. It was a rotten choice."

"Then we could go to my hotel. It's not far from here. It's very modern in style, and not exactly romantic, but it's comfortable. Large bed, good bathroom, room service. And now tell me more about this book *A Room with a View*. Is it translated into German?"

"That is for you to find out."

"I could try to read it in English."

I smiled. Why should he know Forster?

"To be honest, Paul, I don't read much."

"Do you have other interests?"

"Yes, I am an architect. I'm in love with buildings. I'm very interested in Bauhaus. Have you heard of Bauhaus?"

I told him that I had, which was true, but I was not sure if I was keen on it at all. Then I mentally kicked myself for possibly upsetting him by disliking a movement he so admired.

"When we get to the hotel, I'll draw one of the buildings I designed," he said. Then he added, "I will draw it for you."

I had the whole evening and the night free. But how would I explain the drawing to Bruno? The nasty little crime of the heart wriggled inside me like a worm.

"I hope to get to know you better," Heinrich said.

Once in the hotel, which had a discreet opulence, suitable for Florence, we ordered a bottle of wine, plus chicken with salad in a tangy *agrodolce* dressing.

"I hope you are hungry."

I said yes, which I was, but I wanted sex more.

"First I'll have a shower," he said. "Do you want to join me?"

I said that I would wait for him. Heinrich sang in the bathroom, and it was so loud, it almost covered the sound of the water. He had a good voice, and I enjoyed listening to him. I sat on a light brown chair and waited for him. A quarter of an hour later, after he had stopped singing, he opened the bathroom door. I saw that he was dressed only in a black bathrobe. He had washed his blond, slightly curly hair and his face looked strong and very Teutonic. He had deep blue eyes. My desire for him gave me an erection.

"What were you singing?" I asked.

"Hugo Wolf. I like his lieder."

"You have a very beautiful voice."

"I wanted to be a professional singer once, but I loved architecture more. I like straight lines, vertical lines, horizontal lines. That is why I would not be happy in Rome. I see too many curves there. Florence refreshes me and inspires me. It is quiet in its beauty. I think my designs are quiet as well." He paused, then added, "Now I will draw a copy of one of my designs. The building does exist."

At the far end of the room, he opened a folder and took out drawing paper and several pencils. In silence, he sat at a table next to one of the windows, and I watched as his hands deftly moved across the paper. I kept silent and admired his long

116

fingers and the shape of his broad hand as it drew.

"There," he said at last.

As he walked towards me, his bathrobe opened, and I saw the very light brown hair around his genitals. I imagined it to be very soft. His penis nestled neatly, and his balls were tightly rounded. He caught my look, and of all things, he blushed. He closed the robe. Then he handed me the drawing.

It was a square building. At first, I found the shape rather obvious. He had used shades of grey and black, with accents of soft pink for the windows. The windows were mere slits, but the pink colour he used for them added a tenderness to the whole design. Still, there was something slightly medieval about them and I imagined arrows being shot from them.

"But no one can see out through those long very narrow windows."

"It is a library. The interior is bright with light. The students are meant to not look out while they are studying. Nothing outside can distract them from their work."

I told him I liked it, and he said, "It's yours, because you like reading! That's why I chose this specific building for you. I wanted to impress you. I also wanted to impress you, because I find you very handsome. I do not think you will ever look old. And I like your serious look. I can imagine you in this building. A student of life."

I looked down, feeling embarrassed by his words. I sensed he needed a lover, and not just an interlude of sex.

"Maybe I can show the place to you one day. It is not far from Stuttgart where I live."

I looked up at him and said, "This can be our only meeting."

"Are you telling me you already have someone in your life?"

"Yes."

"Oh well, that's life," he replied, and there was sadness in his voice. "I am being selfish, but it is a pity for me."

"Yes. It is a pity. At this moment in time, I feel you would be good for me. By the way, my full name is Jean-Paul. I am half-French."

"I did not sense that. But now I can see it. I make a study of faces. I always think that the English without foreign blood in their veins are a little brutal or uninteresting. My mother is half-Hungarian herself. She lives in Budapest. She knows I am gay, and she would like you."

"I don't know what to say, Heinrich."

"Nothing. We may or we may not have sex, but to be honest, I would prefer to make love to you. But now let us change the subject. We must eat."

He looked down at the food.

"I hope that you will remember this meal," he said.

41

On the way back to Rome, Bruno was silent. He had bad moods, and he was in a bad mood throughout our journey.

"I have something to tell you," I said once we reached his flat.

"*Sono stanco*," he said, heading into the kitchen. He opened a tin of tuna with vegetables. "This is all there is. We need to shop. Tomorrow, we shop."

"Bruno, why weren't you talking to me during the journey?"

"I have just said in Italian that I am tired. Don't you know the most basic Italian words?"

I remained quiet. He served up the tuna and once more there was silence. A very heavy silence. A large fly buzzed around us, and he made angry gestures to frighten it away. In doing so, the plate of food balanced on his lap fell to the floor.

"Open a window!" he shouted. "I don't like flies. They bring disease. I hate them. Look at that one on the wall, big and fat."

I opened the window, and the fly made a quick exit, sensing probably how near death was. I picked up Bruno's plate, cleaned up the mess, and he watched me do all this with a sulky grin on his face. This made me in my turn angry, and I regretted the loss of Heinrich. What the hell was I doing with this sixteen-year-old. A man, a beautiful man wanted me, and I choose this youth over him. Heinrich and I could talk, and it was good to talk. In my luggage I had his drawing which he had put into a tube. My anger grew and I took my own plate as well as his, to the kitchen.

"I was unfaithful to you in Firenze." I blurted the words out, my anger showing. "I met this German, and I liked him."

Then I turned round and looked at Bruno. The grin had gone

from his face. He just stared at me for a while, then he burst out laughing.

"You think this is funny, Bruno? I'm admitting I wanted him. I'm admitting he wanted me."

"Now I feel happy," he replied.

"What the fuck do you mean?"

"Truth is truth, and I will tell you the truth. I did not go to Firenze to see my brother's friend. My brother does not have a friend there. He does not exist. I made this story. I am a good actor, no? I knew you would believe the lie. And you did. I wonder that you did not see through it. All that story about him being hidden away after the flood. It was ridiculous. Look at all the restorations Firenze has. Even in the rain it looks its normal self. It lost a few treasures, but it has too many treasures anyway."

"So Giorgio never existed," I said. I felt giddy. I felt sick. "Make me some coffee, Bruno. I don't feel well."

"Of course."

He made the coffee and handed it to me, saying, "I had a lover there. I had to finish everything with him. And do you know why? For you!"

"But—"

"Drink! Jean-Paul, you look terrible."

I sipped at the drink slowly. I burnt my mouth it was so hot. Then I went over and closed the window. I felt jealous and at the same time relieved. After all, I had had my suspicions while we were there.

"So you did this for me?"

"Yes, for you. *Per sempre.* You do understand that, I hope."

"It means always," and I felt tears in my eyes. I did not want tears, and rubbed them away. "Bruno, you are so young, and yet you say *always*. Do you know what always means?"

He sighed very loudly, and then he took me in his arms. He pressed me close to him, and then he nibbled at my ear.

"I am tired," he said. "I had sex with him all the time I was in Firenze. I wanted to finish it like that. He exhausted me."

I broke away and stared at the walls.

"When did your relationship begin with him?" I asked.

"A year ago. He wanted me to live with him."

"Why didn't you?"

"I'm not sure. I felt it was not right. And there is my brother here. I adore my brother. And I must continue having sex with my brother. Maybe even the three of us together."

"Why not?" I replied, but my mind was in a daze.

"It would be good," then he paused for a moment and added, "He is very handsome and he has a very strong cock. He is part of me—but only a part. You mean as much to me as he does. In life there are very different emotions."

"Yes, Bruno, there are different emotions."

The coffee had cooled down. I drank it in one go. I felt dry inside. I also did not know what to think or what to say.

"Did you feel as good with this man you met as with me?" he asked.

"It was, as you have said, a different emotion."

"Did you feel you wanted him more than me?"

I could not answer that.

"I can see that you are not sure."

"I don't really want to talk about him. I can only say that he prefers Florence to Rome."

Bruno laughed. A coarse loud laugh.

"Jean-Paul, he thinks like a tourist! Beautiful Firenze! Roma, she moves. Firenze, he is static. Who would live without the moving, living Piazza Navona? A palace of a place where everyone can enter and enjoy. *Really* enjoy. It is the most treasured place in Italy."

When we got into bed, he fell asleep immediately. I could not sleep.

For several months I continued living with him, and sometimes I went out alone. And one afternoon I came back earlier than usual, and I saw his brother fucking him. Both of them looked at me, but they did not move apart.

"Join us," Bruno said.

"No thank you. Carry on. Maybe I will watch."

"Maybe? Come on, join us. My brother wants you too. I want us to be complete together."

His brother was good-looking but his eyes were dark and I disliked him. Why is it we dislike in an instant? All I knew was that I had to leave them both to enjoy their pleasure. I sat in the kitchen, closed the door, and pressed my hands against my ears to shut out the loud grunts and cries. I remained there all night. Neither of them came to get me.

The following morning, and they were still in each other's arms asleep. I left the flat. I stayed in a hotel for a week and then rang Heinrich who had given me his number. I told him everything.

"I will come to Italy," he said. "I will be at the same hotel in Florence. Join me there. Promise that you will join me there."

"I promise," I said.

"I will be there the day after tomorrow."

42

Looking back, I see how a whole life can change. As I write this, Heinrich is looking at a book on architecture, sitting by the fire in our flat close to the Piazza della Signoria. Or I should say, his shadowy being is sitting in the chair. He died years ago. I do not want to count them.

43

I arrived in Florence as promised. The sky was blue, and the city was beautiful. I liked it. Why had I disliked it on that visit so many years before with my French lover? One cannot recall everything. Only a fraction of time stores itself in our memory and we make fictions of what we want to believe happened but often did not. These illusions sustain, and the elusive reality of ourselves and others is maintained.

I walked around for a while, then went to the same café where I had joined Bruno for an hour each day. How far away it seemed, although it was only months before. The October sun was not too hot, and I looked towards the Ponte Vecchio. Should I go there and find Heinrich a gift? A souvenir of my return to him? I decided not. The obvious act is often the worst act. I sensed caution was needed and dimmed my own enthusiasm.

I made my way to the hotel. He opened the door, his arms wide. How beautiful he looked in his white suit, his blond hair cut short and the faint smell of an eau de Cologne I could not identify, but which I liked at once. I went to him, and he held me tight. In silence we remained close, and I felt at home.

"I dared to hope," he said.

"I was a fool to return to Rome."

"Decisions cannot be made quickly," he said, leading me to a sofa where we sat side by side.

"I'm afraid I brought nothing but myself," I said.

"We are the same height. Your legs are similar to mine. I have a change of clothes for you. Have a bath. Relax. I brought a record player with me. What composer relaxes you? I have what I think is a small but good collection. Coming here by train was a good idea. I was able to bring a great deal of luggage. While I am here, I will find somewhere for us to live."

"So soon?"

"The sooner the better. I have already made some arrangements in Stuttgart. Now, what music would you like to hear?"

"Do you have any of Mozart's Piano Concertos?"

"I have a few. I like the Ninth, especially. I will put it on for you."

I had my bath, and the suit he gave me to wear was grey and light. In the meantime, he had changed the record to the Twenty-first Piano Concerto.

"How handsome you look," he said.

"Thank you, Heinrich. I just can't believe I am actually here. This isn't the same hotel room, is it?"

"No," and he laughed. "Even rooms change."

"I like this one better," I said. "How fine this October weather is. How the light pours in through all of the windows."

"I have some free time before I return to work. Later I will show you my latest designs. I have had a few commissions and can start up in Florence. Hopefully I will do even better here. I am sure to, if you are with me."

I did not reply. I could not. I looked out of one of the windows and yes, there was the top of the Duomo where we had first met. I pointed this out to Heinrich.

"If I stay with you, I must get down to my writing. I made some notes on the train here, but please do not ask me to reveal anything about it. It is a set of variations; the variations that make our lives so fundamentally bearable and full of illusions."

I wanted to tell him about the drawings of Jesus, John and Judas, but they too were behind me. I had torn them into pieces and thrown them away. The past was the past.

44

I wrote my novel, and it was published. Heinrich became successful in Florence and designed several buildings for the outskirts of the city. As for my book, it sold fairly well, and I started on my second. It was one day when we were walking by the Arno, I asked him something I had never thought of before: his age. Unbelievable as it may seem, we were three years into our relationship, and I was nearly thirty.

"I am fifty-five."

Why hadn't I asked him before? I could not recall a moment when it had ever come to my mind, even on birthdays. I found his body firm, and his face only slightly lined. His blond hair made many people stare at him, and yet he seemed unaware of his good looks. Heinrich had one major virtue, and that was his lack of narcissism.

"But I thought—"

"That I was younger?" he asked, gently reaching out and touching my face.

"I just didn't think of it, Heinrich. Yes, when we first met, I knew you were older, but I put no years onto it, and then, well, it has never come up."

"And yet you have seen my passport."

"I never opened it."

"I confess I opened yours."

I looked at the river, then up at him.

"We have worked hard recently," I said. "Speaking of passports, could we go away together somewhere?"

"How would you like to meet my mother in Budapest? I can arrange for the visas, and I'm sure she would like to meet you."

"I would like that too."

"She is *very* old, but despite some confusion, she still has her wits about her. Like you, she reads a lot, especially in German. My father was German, but she left him before the war and went to Hungary. She also has a passion for poetry. Stefan George especially. She sees nothing of the homoeroticism in his work, but sometimes in my youth she called me Maximin—after the adolescent who became the idol of George's circle. His real name was Maximilian Kronberger, and I suspect he was not worthy of such adoration, but he was like a god to that circle. She also likes Verlaine, Mallarmé, and Baudelaire. Before leaving Germany, she read a lot to me that I was too young to understand."

"Does she know I write?"

"Very much so. In her long letters she has said how happy she is that I have met an intelligent and worthy man."

We continued walking through the streets of Florence, and had coffee in that inevitable tourist spot: the Piazza della Signoria. I pointed out the copy of Michelangelo's *David* to Heinrich.

"Do you think *he* is worth adoration?" I asked.

"No one is worth it," he replied, and as he raised his cup to his lips, I saw his hand tremble. Putting the cup back into the saucer he added, "Adoration is *not* good, but once, yes, I *did* adore something very wrong. I will have that pain for the rest of my life."

I did not ask any more questions and when we returned home, he asked me to fuck him, and for the first time, to strike him—on the back, with my hands. This request shocked me. Nevertheless, I fucked him and then struck him—but not hard enough.

"Harder," he cried out. "Punish me!"

"No, I can't do it," I said, and got up off the bed.

"You will. You must. You must love me enough to punish me."

45

I went with him to Budapest, and despite the beautiful views of Buda from across the river, I found it heavy and I disliked the city. He took me to an ancient sauna, rich, he said in its history, and there, on a slab of stone, he laid out naked and once again asked me to beat his body. I straddled his prone flesh, and with the rhythmic beating of my hands, succeeded in making him cry out.

"More, more," he said.

A small crowd of men looked on, and feeling ashamed of the exhibition we were making, I felt angry, and beat him harder until his back was marked with the blows. Some of the men laughed, others just stared or gossiped together.

"I will never do that again," I said as we left the place.

"You will," he replied.

"But why?"

He did not answer my question, and said, "Mother is waiting for us. We have been here for two days, and I needed that respite before seeing her. Communication by post is good, but face to face I am not sure I want to see her."

"You love her."

"I loved my father more. And that has always been a problem between her and me. Her name is Magda, by the way. Please call her that. Never call her by my father's name, Friedrich Schiller, like the writer. She even dislikes Schiller's plays. Be sure not to mention him."

"Why should I? I've never read any of his plays."

"Good."

"Is her dislike of this writer solely down to him sharing your surname?"

"Yes."

I paused before asking, "Why did you ask me to do that to you in the sauna? I told you before that I would not."

"I believe you love me more and more each day, and that eventually you will understand that it is normal for me. Remember, I told you before that it is a punishment?"

"But for what?" I cried out.

We were on the Pest side, and he found a taxi. Inside we said nothing to each other, and after tearing through what seemed like an endless maze of streets, the taxi eventually stopped.

"This is the house?" the taxi driver asked in Hungarian.

"Yes." Heinrich got out first, and the man was paid.

As the taxi drove away, Heinrich put some money into my black overcoat. It was cold in Budapest.

"That is in case you see anything you want," he said and then opened the gate to the property. Spread out before us was a broad drive, and at the top, an imposing house, pink in colour and elaborately decorated with images of flowers and green foliage. It seemed to me that Magda had created her own world to live in. Heinrich rang the bell. An old woman opened the door.

"Good evening, Else. Is my mother expecting us?" Heinrich asked. She nodded in reply, without smiling, first to Heinrich, then to me.

"I will take you to her," she said. "You never remember the way."

"Naturally, Else. I never come here."

We climbed a flight of stairs. The walls were covered with paintings.

"She rescued some of the artists that Hitler hated," Heinrich said.

Then we entered a vast room with a wide fireplace, a blazing fire, and again more paintings on the red walls. Most of the furniture was also a deep, rich red, and in one chair, I saw her. Her face was beautiful, given her age, and silently she beckoned to us. We went over and she held out her hand to

Heinrich who bowed to her and kissed it. She then held her hand out to me. Hesitant, but not surprised, I kissed her hand also. In the rather sombre light of the room I saw few wrinkles, few marks of her declining years.

"Please call me Magda," she said, and smiled at me. Then she turned to Heinrich and commented on how well he looked.

"Bring some chairs close to me," she asked.

Heinrich brought two upright chairs, finely designed and made of wood. Red cushions were on each of them. We sat down.

"So, this is the man you love, Heinrich," she said without any hesitation.

"Yes, mother, I love him."

"May I call you Jean-Paul?" she asked me.

"Please do," I replied.

From that moment on, we talked of many things, and inevitably poetry came into the discussion. Heinrich averted his head when this happened.

"Mother, may I use the bathroom?" he asked at one point.

"You know your way."

"Do I?" he asked and looked perplexed.

"Your memory is going, my son. It is on this floor, along the corridor."

He left us alone together, and Magda beamed at me.

"At last, he has had the tact to leave us alone."

"He is tactful," I replied.

"And do you truly love him?" she asked, and I noticed a twinkle in her faded blue eyes.

"Yes, very much."

"Despite his past?" she murmured.

At first, I did not hear the question and I bent forward. She repeated what she had said.

"My son wants to be punished for the past. It is his need. Does this disturb you?"

"I'm sorry, but—"

"Clearly you must know he needs it."

130

"Yes," I replied reluctantly.

"But you don't know why," she paused, and I shook my head.

"After the war, he killed someone. The communists had taken over. He was very young, and of course previous to that, he had been a soldier serving under Hitler. It was in a deserted place. In that ruined landscape Berlin had become. A drunken communist and another man forced him to the ground and violated him. They did it in turn. They said they were doing it in the name of Stalin."

I was silent. Was I shocked? I cannot remember. I recalled Bruno and his descriptions of men being shot in the head. I shuddered.

"Did he kill one of them?"

"Yes, and he mutilated the other with a knife. I cannot believe it, but I do believe it. You see, before the war began, I shut myself away. Poetry saved me from going insane. He came to me later, much later, and he confessed to me. He said that he did it in a state of furious passion. What sort of passion is it that drives a man to kill?"

"If you want a serious answer, I think it is man's burden," I replied. "Man has a great capacity to kill the human being in us, and those men tried to kill the human being in Heinrich."

"Yes. You are right." After a while, she said, "I had to tell you. I know he wanted me to tell you. He made that clear to me in a letter."

"Can you tell me something else? Did Heinrich support Hitler? Or did he somehow subvert or rebel? Some soldiers did."

"Who knows what was in his heart. I don't know. I never will know. His youth was painful because he dreaded people finding out that he was attracted to men. His desires would have cost him his life if revealed during that period. I like to think that things have improved, but even now, acts of hatred are committed against men who love men, and anyone who is different. The man he killed told him that once the communists ruled the earth, he would be executed for his *perversion*."

"I am shocked."

"But please, please Jean-Paul, you must continue to love him. I fear he will always need punishment for what he did, but fundamentally, he is a good man."

Heinrich returned. He looked at both of us, then he stared at me.

"You know?" he asked.

"Yes, I know," I replied, and somehow I held out my hand to him.

Magda stared on, a smile on her face.

"Have you read Stefan George?" she asked. Then, before I could reply she lowered her head and said, "Am I lucky to be still alive? I have seen the Nazis, the revolt of 1956, and now communism. I have seen it all."

46

All those years ago. I stared at his invisible presence. Nothing had changed in our home. I was about to put down my pen when I recalled a dream I had had the night before.

I awoke and my heart felt nailed with the truth, seeing again what I had seen in my sleep. All the men, all the youths in my life were with me, and naked they stood against a grey wall. I could only call out their names, one by one; the litany of names, their faces forgotten. A cold wind blew in this space I stood in, and only a tree, a purple beech, sheltered me for a while. Then I was swept by a sudden gust towards them, and I was naked too, joining them without memory, in their stillness and their lost passions.

******